Zane O'Sullivan, Julia Thought, Her Heart Pounding. In The Flesh.

He hunkered down to where her car had slid into the ditch. "Helluva place to park," he drawled, his tone as dry as the summer road.

That smoke-and-whiskey voice had always unsettled her—made her pulse beat a little quicker, her breath come a little shallower. A decade later, that hadn't changed.

But some things *had* changed. Defined by a close-fitting T-shirt, his chest was broader, deeper, stronger. His face looked leaner, his cheekbones more sharply chiseled, and a network of well-etched lines radiated beyond his sunglasses.

Those lines deepened, as if he'd narrowed his gaze. "You okay? You look a bit stunned."

He straightened to open her door, and she quickly looked away, but not quickly enough to avoid an eyeful of denim-encased male groin. Suddenly she felt more than stunned. She felt breathless, dizzy.

The heat, she told herself…

Dear Reader,

What could be more satisfying than the sinful yet guilt-free pleasure of enjoying six new passionate, powerful and provocative Silhouette Desire romances this month?

Get started with *In Blackhawk's Bed*, July's MAN OF THE MONTH and the latest title in the SECRETS! miniseries by Barbara McCauley. *The Royal & the Runaway Bride* by Kathryn Jensen—in which the heroine masquerades as a horse trainer and becomes a princess—is the seventh exciting installment in DYNASTIES: THE CONNELLYS, about an American family that discovers its royal roots.

A single mom melts the steely defenses of a brooding ranch hand in *Cowboy's Special Woman* by Sara Orwig, while a detective with a secret falls for an innocent beauty in *The Secret Millionaire* by Ryanne Corey. A CEO persuades a mail-room employee to be his temporary wife in the debut novel *Cinderella & the Playboy* by Laura Wright, praised by *New York Times* bestselling author Debbie Macomber as "a wonderful new voice in Silhouette Desire." And in *Zane: The Wild One* by Bronwyn Jameson, the mayor's daughter turns up the heat on the small town's bad boy made good.

So pamper the romantic in you by reading all six of these great new love stories from Silhouette Desire!

Enjoy!

Joan Marlow Golan

Joan Marlow Golan
Senior Editor, Silhouette Desire

Please address questions and book requests to:
Silhouette Reader Service
U.S.: 3010 Walden Ave., P.O. Box 1325, Buffalo, NY 14269
Canadian: P.O. Box 609, Fort Erie, Ont. L2A 5X3

Zane: The Wild One
BRONWYN JAMESON

™ Silhouette®

Desire®

Published by Silhouette Books

America's Publisher of Contemporary Romance

SILHOUETTE BOOKS

ISBN 0-373-76452-9

ZANE: THE WILD ONE

Copyright © 2002 by Bronwyn Turner

This edition published by arrangement with Harlequin Books S.A.

® and TM are trademarks of Harlequin Books S.A., used under license. Trademarks indicated with ® are registered in the United States Patent and Trademark Office, the Canadian Trade Marks Office and in other countries.

Visit Silhouette at www.eHarlequin.com

Printed in U.S.A.

Books by Bronwyn Jameson

Silhouette Desire

In Bed with the Boss's Daughter #1380
Addicted to Nick #1410
Zane: The Wild One #1452

BRONWYN JAMESON

spent much of her childhood with her head buried in a book. As a teenager, she discovered romance novels, and it was only a matter of time before she turned her love of reading them into a love of writing them. Bronwyn shares an idyllic piece of the Australian farming heartland with her husband and three sons, a thousand sheep, a dozen horses, assorted wildlife and one kelpie dog. She still chooses to spend her limited downtime with a good book. Bronwyn loves to hear from readers. Write to her at bronwyn@bronwynjameson.com.

For my boys—thanks for your support, your humor, your insight into the male psyches and the coffee. I love you all.

One

It wasn't like in the movies.

The action didn't cut to slow motion as her tires lost traction in the loose gravel, sending the car into a wildly slewing fishtail. The camera didn't zoom to closeup as she wrestled for control of the wheel. There was no sense of time standing still. No sudden clarity of thought, sound, motion. No if-onlys.

One second Julia Goodwin was proceeding at her usual sensible speed, midway through the twelve-mile drive from her home in Plenty to her sister's country property; the next she came upon a trio of magpies directly in her path. And seemingly the next second after that she was sitting there, steering wheel clutched in a death grip, going nowhere. In between there had undoubtedly been some swerving, slewing and wrestling, but not much thinking.

Finally she opened her eyes—to the sight of a kangaroo loping through the summer-dry grass that edged the unsealed road. The big grey stopped and lifted its head to scent the air.

"Now if *you* had been sitting on the road, big guy, I'd have had reason to take evasive action." As the animal bounded gracefully over a fence and disappeared from sight, she shook her head in self-reproach. During countless driving lessons, many along this same road, she'd been told never to swerve for wildlife. To slow down, hit the horn and let them do their own evading.

Except Julia would never risk hurting any living thing, birds included. So she had closed her eyes, braked hard *and* swerved, all of which had probably contributed to her current predicament...and being stuck in this particular roadside ditch was definitely a predicament.

Because she loved the view from the top of Quilty's Hill, she'd taken the back road to Chantal's, and it wasn't called "the back road" for nothing. Passing traffic was...well...there wasn't any.

Still, it appeared she had survived the sudden stop in one piece. Shifting gingerly in her seat, she wriggled her legs, moved her neck one way and then the other. Her head didn't fall off, and that had to be a plus. Finger by finger she unglued her hands from the wheel and, despite a bad case of the tremors, she managed to both straighten her sunglasses and release her seat belt.

It took longer to deal with the door latch and when she tried to stand, her legs collapsed from under her. Fine. The situation could be assessed as easily from ground level. In fact from this angle she could see exactly why she wasn't going anywhere.

The car had come to rest—in the loosest sense of the phrase—on the rim of a table drain. If she had been driving her father's Mercedes instead of her mother's hatchback, it would have resembled a beached whale. High and dry and immovable. The gurgling and hissing coming from under the hood might indicate radiator damage, and now she looked more closely the front tire appeared flattish.

But, it could have been much worse. Julia herself had escaped uninjured. For the moment.

Heaven knows what harm would befall her when she didn't show up for Chantal's dinner party. Her sister hated uneven numbers, not to mention how the whole shebang had been constructed around her presence. Because Julia needed a husband. Because Julia never went anywhere to meet the "right kind of man." Because no man or machine could stop Chantal when she was on a mission, and Mission: Marry Julia had assumed top priority since New Year's.

It wasn't that she didn't appreciate Chantal's efforts or her motivation. Purely and simply, her sister would do anything to make her happy, even if that meant acting in direct contradiction to her own beliefs. Marriage, according to Chantal, invited heartache. Career, on the other hand, provided respect, challenge and fulfillment.

Julia didn't agree. She had been married once, and if they hadn't followed Paul's career to Sydney, if she hadn't hated the isolated loneliness of big-city living—and if he hadn't gone and fallen in love with another woman—she would likely still *be* married.

For better or for worse.

Because despite her parents' lofty ambitions, despite her siblings's stellar success, despite all the vocational testing and you-can-do-so-much-more-with-your-life advice, Julia had never wanted anything *except* to be married, to make a home and a garden and the babies she knew would fill the empty corners of her soul.

Unfortunately the children she had yet to have weren't going to help her out of this fix. Fortunately her legs now felt as if they were up to supporting her, especially if she got rid of the three-inch heels borrowed from her housemate, Kree. And the stockings. And the slip that clung to her legs like seal-wrap.

That done, she made her way to the center of the road and looked around. There wasn't a lot to see. Enough roadside eucalypts to make her grateful the drain had stopped her progress, and a century-old fence that wouldn't have stopped a bicycle's progress. Behind her stretched acres of rolling grassland, punctuated with the scattered dots of grazing cattle and bisected by the curling ribbon of road she had just driven down. Ahead, uncleared scrub marked the start of the Tibbaroo Nature Reserve.

Drat. She couldn't have picked a more isolated spot. The nearest farmhouse was miles away, and already she could feel both sharp-edged gravel and the baked-in heat of a long summer day biting into her soles. She shifted her weight from one foot to the other as she pondered which would be perceived as the most stupid course of action. A: walking several miles in bare feet. B: walking the same distance in stilettos. Or C: waiting for help.

A low persistent buzz permeated her thoughts and she swatted at the lone fly circling her head. The fly decamped, but the buzz persisted. Julia groaned as she identified Option D as the correct answer to her question.

The most stupid course of action would be forgetting her mother's car phone.

She picked her way back to the car, slid into the driver's seat and rescued the squawking instrument.

"Julia? Where in heaven's name are you?" It sounded as if Chantal had worked up a full head of steam. "I know I said seven-thirty, but you're usually early, and I need you to fix this cursed sauce. I followed your recipe, but something's not work—"

"Actually," Julia managed to interject, "I've had an accident of sorts."

"Are you all right?"

"Yes. I'm fine, but the car—"

"Oh, my God, you didn't mangle Mother's car?"

"No, it's not damaged. Much." She closed her eyes and crossed her fingers, although it wasn't really a lie. "But it's going to need towing."

Julia gave her location, and Chantal swung straight into organizational mode. That was, after all, her forte.

"With all this food on the go, I can't come and get you, but I'll send Dan as soon as he gets here."

"Dan?"

"He's a new dentist in Cliffton. He seems a little on the quiet side, so do try to get him talking. I'm sure you'll find plenty in common if you give him a chance."

He's a little dull, so you two will get along famously, Julia translated.

"Just sit tight and wait. Oh, and I'll call a tow truck."

"It's Friday night. Please, don't drag Bill out." But she was talking to dead air. Everything organized to her satisfaction, Chantal had hung up.

With her gaze fixed on the rearview mirror, Julia saw the tow truck crest Quilty's Hill, then zoom in and out of sight as it traversed the winding descent.

"Where's the fire?" she murmured, sitting up straighter and pushing her dark glasses to the top of her head.

Fast wasn't like old Bill. The laconic garage owner typified the pace of the small town that had been home for most of Julia's life. But old Bill owned the only tow truck in Plenty, drove the only tow truck in Plenty....

Except on those rare occasions when Zane O'Sullivan was in town.

By the time the truck rocked to a halt, Julia's heart was pounding. The pall of dust that had trailed the vehicle down the hill caught up with its quarry, circled, then settled in a thick brown shroud. Dry-mouthed, Julia heard the thunk of a closing door, the crunch of brittle herbage under heavy boots, and then he was right there, anchoring hands spread wide on the roof as he hunkered down to her open window.

Zane O'Sullivan. In the flesh.

"Helluva place to park your car," he drawled, his tone as dry as the summer road.

That smoke-and-whisky voice had always unsettled Julia—made her pulse beat a little quicker, her breath come a little shallower—but it usually didn't render her incapable of speech...but then, usually she only encountered it on the distant end of a phone line. In fact, this was the first time Kree's footloose brother had ever spoken to her face-to-face.

Back in high school she had found his shining good looks and tarnished bad attitude so contradictory, so intimidating, that she had literally fled from any chance encounter. More than a decade later, and some things hadn't changed. Up close, Zane O'Sullivan still unnerved her—although now that she had regained her equilibrium, she noticed that some things *had* changed after all.

Defined by a close-fitting white T-shirt, his chest was definitely broader, deeper, stronger. His hair was the same sun-tinged blend of honey and gold, still worn longer than regulation, still finger-combed back from his broad forehead. His face looked leaner, his cheekbones more sharply chiselled, and a network of well-etched lines radiated beyond his aviator shades.

Those squint lines deepened as if he had narrowed his gaze. "You okay? You look a bit stunned."

He straightened to open her door, and she quickly looked away, but not quickly enough to avoid an eyeful of denim-encased male groin. Suddenly she felt more than stunned. She felt breathless, dizzy. The heat, she reasoned, as she hastily slapped her own sunglasses into place.

As if they could dim such glaring good looks. A hundred pair and she would still be mesmerized. A picture formed in her giddy head—her, pulling on pair after pair of sunglasses, one on top of the other, in a vain attempt to dilute his male beauty—and she laughed out loud. The laughter evaporated when she realized how loony her behavior must seem to a bystander.

She turned in her seat to find the only spectator frowning down at her. One hand rested on the door frame; his long fingers drummed an impatient beat. He looked as though he wished he were somewhere else. Anywhere else. Good grief, she hadn't said a word in the several minutes since he'd arrived, hadn't answered his concerned question.

"I'm fine." She swung her head from side to side. "See? No visible signs of head injury."

He didn't look convinced. In fact, as she slid out from behind the wheel, he looked downright bemused. Best to get the towing sorted out before he decided she truly was crazy and made good his escape.

"I'm not sure how much damage I've done. See this tire? I expect it's ruined, and I hit the ditch pretty hard so I could have broken the steering and who knows what underneath. Oh, and it boiled. Do you think the radiator's damaged?"

"Could be." He didn't even glance at the car. "You sure you didn't bump your head on the steering wheel?"

"I might have a touch of the sun or delayed shock or something, but otherwise I'm in excellent shape."

He continued to study her, so fixedly that she wondered

if some football-size bump had appeared on her head. But then she felt a tingling heat in the pit of her stomach and she knew he wasn't looking at bumps on her head.

He was checking out the bumps on her body.

She should have left the slip on. No—she shouldn't have let Kree hustle her into wearing this dress in the first place. On Kree it looked benign, but then Kree was a good three inches shorter than Julia's five-seven. And Kree didn't have hips...or much else in the way of bumps.

"On your way to a party?"

"Yes. At my sister's," she replied with forced brightness. "You remember Claire Heaslip? Well, Chantal leased her grandfather's block last year."

Too much information. Too much *thoughtless* information. As if he would have forgotten Claire Heaslip. Even if the rumors weren't altogether true.

"Do you usually go in bare feet?" he asked evenly, obviously choosing to ignore her comment.

"Hardly."

Her laughter mixed amusement with discomfort—discomfort caused by both the Claire Heaslip gaffe and her heated response to his gaze on her legs, on skin laid bare by the dress's abbreviated hemline.

"Chantal would have a stroke if I turned up barefoot. I took them off because I was contemplating walking." She retreated to the far side of the car and retrieved the shoes from the passenger seat, grimacing as she slipped them on. "These are not your ideal walking shoes."

No kidding, his silence seemed to say. To a man dressed functionally in jeans, T-shirt and boots, her cocktail ensemble probably looked way over the top. Which it suddenly felt. While she silently bemoaned her lack of judgement in trusting Kree's fashion advice, Zane went into work mode, studying the lay of the car, fetching the truck.

Before he hooked it up, he glanced her way. "You want me to drop you at your sister's before I start here?"

"No. Chantal said she would send someone."

Not just anyone, but Dan the Dentist, handpicked as suitable husband material. She pictured him in a sober suit and tie, brown hair neatly parted and combed into place, and she imagined the evening ahead, as flat and colourless as that image.

She looked at Zane O'Sullivan and one word came to mind. *Technicolor.* Before she could think of all the reasons why she shouldn't, she took a deep breath and spoke quickly. "I've changed my mind. Could I hitch a ride back to town with you? Would you mind?"

He gave her a look, which, between those shades and the straight set of his mouth, she found impossible to read. "Doesn't matter if I mind or not. I'm not leaving you out here."

Ten minutes later Zane cursed his sense of chivalry. Enjoying the thought of what she could or could not possibly be wearing under that silky wisp of a dress was one thing. Thinking about taking it off her was another altogether. She was Principal Goodwin's daughter, *Mayor* Goodwin's daughter, for Pete's sake. Definitely not the kind of woman you imagined naked.

Not in the way he was contemplating. With those fey hazel eyes warm with wanting, all that dark glossy hair cloaking his pillow, and those generous curves covered only in smooth pale skin...and him.

Hoo, man.

Zane shook the heat from his vision, then attempted to apply all his attention to the road. But how could he concentrate with the hint of her perfume—something as softly fragrant as a spring dawn—drifting in and out of his senses? Not to mention how she kept peeping looks at him from behind her dark glasses. Another five minutes of this and he would likely break out in a sweat. Or do something dumb, like invite her for a drink. Or something truly moronic like skipping the drink and taking her straight to his room.

He almost snorted out loud. Julia Goodwin's expensive finery decorating the floor of his cheap hotel room? Keep dreaming, bud!

"I'm sorry I dragged you out," she said eventually in her softly voiced, carefully phrased way. "No doubt there are places you would rather be on a Friday night."

She had that right, but the one uppermost in his mind— his room, his bed—he kept to himself. "Yeah, but I doubt the Lion'll run dry before I get back."

"You were having a drink?"

"I was about to. Bill had already had several when he got your sister's message."

"So that's why you're here." He felt her studying him, more openly this time. "Thank you."

Zane shrugged. "It's my job."

"No, it's Bill's job. I know you help him out whenever you're in town...."

Her voice trailed off, inviting him to answer her unasked question about what brought him to town. Why not? Talking to her was safer than fantasising about her. "I've got a week or so to kill, so I thought I'd give Bill a break and see how Kree's doing."

"She didn't mention you were coming."

"Last-minute decision."

"Oh. Have you seen her yet?"

"I only got in this afternoon and figured she'd be busy. Besides, I'm never at my best in a hair shop."

"Don't let Kree catch you referring to her salon as a

hair shop," she said with a smile, which froze almost instantly. "Although I wish you *had* gone in, because now you've missed her. She's gone away for the weekend with Tagg. Her boyfriend. He lives over in Cliffton."

"Then I'll see her when she gets back. How is she?"

"She's Kree." The smile returned. "Busy, full-on, happy."

"You mean, manic?"

Her smile grew to a soft appreciative chuckle, and Zane found himself turning to catch the laughter on her face. It transformed her from pretty to stunning, and he found himself staring—again—and wondering how he never noticed that before, back when he lived in Plenty.

Probably because he'd never been close enough to see her laughing. Hell, he remembered times when she had crossed the street to avoid him, and if she ever *had* looked his way, it was with the kind of curious, wide-eyed fascination usually reserved for viewing aliens. Which pretty much summed up how this town had always made him feel.

Right now he felt her watching him with a different kind of fascination. She had gone very still, the laughter fading from her lips. Her focus seemed to shift to his mouth. His lips tingled with heat. Uh-uh, no way. She was the dinner-and-dating-and-home-to-meet-Daddy type, not the straight-into-bed type. And absolutely not the front-seat-of-the-truck type.

He dragged his eyes back to the road and his mind back from the gutter, pressed a touch harder on the accelerator and searched for a diversionary topic of conversation.

"You're all dressed up to party." He waved a hand in the general direction of her itty-bitty dress. "So why did you decide to go home, instead?"

"I didn't really want to go in the first place." She

shifted her shoulders uneasily. "Do you think running my car off the road is a good enough excuse to cancel? I mean, it's not as if I crashed, or hurt myself…."

"Why do you need an excuse? If you didn't want to go, you should've said no."

"Chantal doesn't recognize the word."

"Maybe she needs to hear it more often."

A small frown puckered her brow, and Zane wondered how right he'd got that. Then he told himself it wasn't his problem. That wasn't why he had asked her about the party. He was making small talk, that was all. He absolutely did not want to know if, for example, she was letting down some suit-and-tie type by not turning up.

"Back when you were hooking up to the car, I rang Chantal to say I'd decided to go home. She didn't sound happy. I suspect she might send someone to fetch me."

"If you weren't at home, that someone wouldn't be able to fetch you."

"Not home?" Her softly incredulous laugh brought his gaze back to her mouth, made him think of intimacies he had no business with. "In case it escaped your attention, there are not a lot of hidey-holes open on a Friday night in Plenty."

"There's the Lion. You could come down for a drink, shoot some pool," Zane suggested casually, not because he expected her to accept. Not because he wanted her to accept. For a long moment she stared at him, surprised, but obviously considering his invitation. He felt his body quicken. Then she shook her head and looked down at her hands, folded neatly in her lap.

"Thanks, but I think I'll have to pass this time."

This time. As if he was in the habit of asking her every other day. But as he downshifted to cross the railway line, he shrugged and cut her a look. "Your loss."

Julia looked out the window. They had reached the edge of town. In a couple of minutes she would step down from the truck, toss him a careless "See you later" and know that later might be another twelve years. She felt a deep, totally inappropriate sense of disappointment. Her loss indeed.

Of course, she could always change into some jeans and walk down to the Lion. She could saunter up alongside him and say, "Hey, Zane. You want to shoot some pool?"

Then she could watch the whole bar population either A: burst into spontaneous laughter, B: keel over with shock, or C: call for the men in white coats.

Julia Goodwin sauntering up to a public bar? That isn't going to happen, she concluded fatalistically as he turned the corner into Bower Street and pulled up alongside number fourteen. When he reached for his door, she leaned across to stop him. "There's no need to get out."

She felt him still, and when his gaze dropped to where her hand rested on his forearm, she was suddenly aware of more than his stillness. His skin felt warm—no, *hot*— and slightly rough, with its smattering of hair. It also felt incredibly hard, and she realized with a start how long it had been since she had touched a man's bare skin. And how much she missed that sensation of heat and strength, of leashed masculine power.

The moment stretched out, silent and thick with awareness, until she reclaimed her hand, dragging her fingers a little because she couldn't stop herself. Telltale heat rose from her neck to her ears, and she silently thanked Kree for making her leave her hair down. At least she had got that part right!

She cleared her throat, unable to look at him in case he had misinterpreted that touch as some sort of come-on. "I just wanted to say thank you, and sorry for interrupting your night, and I hope you catch up with Kree soon.''

"I'll call her at work on Monday."

"Mornings are usually quietest, especially Monday. She might even be able to take a half day." She reached for the door. "See you later, then."

"What about your car?"

Julia blinked, and he hooked a thumb back over his shoulder.

Ah, that car! How could she have forgotten? "It's my mother's, actually. I don't have a car at the moment, so she loaned me hers while she's overseas. My parents are in Tuscany." And why am I telling him all this? She clutched her evening bag with unsteady fingers. "What did you need to know about the car?"

"D'you want Bill to fix whatever needs fixing, or just do up a quote?"

"Oh. Yes."

"Yes…what?" he asked slowly, and she felt that same intense scrutiny she had felt out by the roadside. Her ears burned with heat as she scrambled for an answer to the simple question.

"Yes, please." *Good grief, could she have said anything more stupid?* She bit her lip, then tried again. "Yes. Please have him fix whatever needs fixing. Bill does all our work—there's no need for a quote."

Quitting on that positively eloquent note seemed like a good plan, so she opened her door and slid down to the curb, but before she closed the door she forced herself to smile up at him. "I really can't thank you enough for bringing me home."

"You'll get the bill."

Julia shook her head. "I wanted to thank *you*, personally."

"Buy me a drink sometime."

She stared up at him, one part of her brain screaming, *How about now?* while another urged her to smile, offer something politely meaningless such as, *Yes, we must do that sometime,* and walk away.

Oh, but she didn't want to listen to that safe, sensible, good-girl voice. For once she wanted to do something a little bit bad. Ordinarily one drink wouldn't qualify as even vaguely bad, but she had a strong feeling—a hot, dizzying feeling—that a drink with Zane O'Sullivan wouldn't be ordinary.

"I think I would like..." She shifted her weight from one foot to the other, moistened her lips, then realized she had lost his attention. He was frowning into his side mirror, while his fingers drummed against the wheel.

"Looks like you have a visitor."

She stepped back just far enough to see the gleaming white Volvo that had pulled up behind them, and the gleamingly groomed man who stepped from the driver's seat. He looked solid and respectable and, yes, dull.

She heard the tow truck kick over and felt such a jolt of panic, she had to stop herself from leaping at the window. Instead she stepped onto the running board and somehow above the thud of her heart she heard herself say, "I really would like to buy you that drink sometime."

Perhaps he saw the nervous tension in her face. Or perhaps he was looking right by her at Dan the Dentist waiting patiently on the verge. With those impenetrable lenses, it was impossible to know. Whatever he saw, it caused one corner of his mouth to kick up wryly. It also caused him to shake his head and say, "Thanks, but I'm thinking that's not such a great idea after all."

Of course he was right.

She stepped down from the window and away from the

truck, and as she watched it pull away, she felt a weighty gloom settle over her.

Drinks with Zane O'Sullivan might not be such a great idea, but that didn't make a dinner party with Mr. Solid and Respectable sound any more palatable.

Two

In the end she didn't go to Chantal's dinner party. Instead she shared a considerably less formal supper, sitting at her kitchen table, with Dan. He wasn't as dull as she had imagined. In fact, he seemed nice, in a comfy, companionable way. When he sheepishly admitted that Chantal had browbeaten him into attending her party, Julia decided she could like him.

She certainly liked how her concentration remained fixed on the conversation, instead of straying to his lips. She enjoyed the complete absence of breathlessness and butterflies, and she positively loved how she could read every expression on his open face.

If she ever went for a drink with Dan she wouldn't consider it bad, and touching his arm would be simply that. Touching his arm. It wouldn't remind her how long it had been since a man's arms embraced her, or how many nights she lay awake wondering if she would ever be held that closely again.

If Dan reminded her of a mild autumn morning next to Zane O'Sullivan's midday summer heat, then so much the better. Summer had never been her favorite season.

After she waved Dan goodbye, she told herself she liked a man who fit her homely decor, as Dan surely did. As Zane wouldn't. *He* would fill her kitchen with his size and his maleness. He definitely would not look at home. Nor would he succumb to Chantal's velvet-steamroller tactics, as Dan had done, although that was a moot point.

His name would never grace one of Chantal's guest lists. For a start, he dressed for work in rugged denim instead of fine Italian suit cloth, and second, he didn't have a prestigious address. In fact, if he even owned a home, Kree hadn't mentioned it. He lived wherever his work as a heavy-machinery mechanic took him—most recently the mines in remote West Australia—and he didn't stay anywhere long. His seven years in Plenty had probably been the longest he had lived in one place.

As she propped open her bedroom window and breathed the heady scent of moonlight and roses, Julia recalled how the O'Sullivan family arrived in town. What a stir they'd created in the conservative community—two rebellious preteens and their mother, old before her time and carrying more baggage than could ever fit in the beat-up van that died slap-bang in the middle of Main Street.

That was how they arrived, and they'd stayed because they couldn't afford to leave.

Julia remembered the hushed talk—ugly rumors of a shadowy strife-filled past—and she remembered how most of the township had ostracized them. A smaller part had adopted them as its charity du jour. Not an easy introduction to a new community, especially for adolescents, and they'd each handled it differently.

Kree had built a brash facade, stuck her snub nose high in the air and refused to accept that she couldn't belong. She battled to win not only acceptance but popularity, too, while her brother…well…Zane never won any popularity contests, because he'd refused to enter.

Some said he would have joined his father behind bars if Bill hadn't given him a job at the garage, first pumping gas after school and then full-time. But as soon as he completed his apprenticeship he'd left Plenty—and those Claire Heaslip rumors—behind.

It seemed as if he had been moving ever since.

Why he'd chosen that lifestyle was not her concern, Julia told herself as she settled into bed and punched her pillow into shape. She had no business thinking of Zane O'Sullivan at all. She should be thinking of Dan—nice, comfortable, settled Dan—who had left with a promise to call her during the week.

Unfortunately, with her eyes closed and the summer air embracing her in its sultry caress, the mild dentist didn't stand a chance. Instead she remembered the supple strength of a man's arm beneath her fingers, the movement of snug white cotton over the casual shrug of broad shoulders, hair glinting with gold in the sun's dusky light.

And with startling clarity she recalled one simple scrap of conversation.

Zane had been hooking the truck to her car when he'd asked how it ended up in the drain. When she told him the sequence of events, magpies and all, he didn't shake his head critically or fix her with the scathing look she'd expected. He simply murmured, "Accidents happen," and carried on with his task.

Julia slipped from wakefulness into sleep with that neutral, nonjudgmental phrase in her mind and a small smile on her lips.

Six days later, Zane stood on the neatly mown verge outside 14 Bower Street, juggling her car keys from one hand to the other. Distracted first by the touch of her hand and then by the arrival of Volvo Man, he had barely glanced sideways at the place on Friday night. Today he saw the truth of Kree's excited exclamation when she had moved in last summer.

"You wouldn't recognize the old Plummer place!" she had practically screamed down the phone line.

A gross understatement, Zane decided.

Julia had transformed the rundown weatherboard cottage, painting it some soft shade of blue and framing it with a garden. He wasn't big on descriptive labels, but right after pretty and peaceful, he thought of welcoming. He could almost imagine the old house itself smiling gently as it opened its arms and beckoned, Come on in.

Houses with arms? Houses that beckoned?

"Time you started sleeping nights, O'Sullivan," he muttered as he turned to study the wider streetscape. It registered that number fourteen wasn't the only recent renovation in the low-rent street…although it was likely the only one resurrected personally by, and now inhabited by, a woman who belonged up on the hill.

He resisted the impulse to look that way. He hated the bitter, edgy feeling in his gut from just thinking about looking up there. It made him want to jump in his car—*any* car—and put pedal to metal. To keep on driving until Plenty was nothing but a hell of a bad memory.

But he didn't, and he wouldn't. Not in her car, anyway.

Although, juggling her keys from hand to hand, he still considered leaving. Suddenly his reason for being there seemed more like an excuse, and a transparent one at that. He should have left a message on her answering machine telling her to collect the car on her way to work. She walked by the garage at eight forty-five every morning, her body swaying enticingly beneath the black skirt and white blouse that were the staff uniform of the town's only department store. He tried not to notice the swaying, but he was only human.

Hell, he didn't even have to leave a message. Tomorrow he could call out to her, "Hey, Julia. Your car's ready."

Except he was here now, and so was she. Zane had seen her go by on her way home, and something about the way she held her head or swung her hips or, shoot, didn't even glance in his direction, had him deciding to return her car. Personally.

Plus, he needed to reassure himself about a couple of things. Such as the way he must have misread that curling caress of her fingers and the message in her eyes when she'd said she wanted to buy him that drink. Such as the way nothing about the impression she had left on his hormones matched his memory of Julia Goodwin, the all-'round good girl who used to cross the street to avoid him. Such as the fact that she already had Volvo Man ready and no doubt willing to take her up on the drinks offer.

Yeah, all he needed was a quick dose of reassurance and he would be on his way. No sweat.

He pocketed the keys, opened the tiny front gate and was ducking under a naturally sculpted archway of climbing roses when a dog appeared…although it took him an instant to recognize it as a dog. The animal appeared as an unidentified black-and-white streak careering through a mass of flowers to his right; then it came into focus as a border collie just before it launched into a frenzied welcome of circling, barking, leaping and grinning.

Zane couldn't help grinning back, even as he tried to temper the dog's exuberance. Then a tingly sense of awareness skittered down his right side and he knew she was there, watching him. Slowly he straightened, turned and immediately found her. Standing in that wild riot of garden, her light sundress lifting with a subtle shift of the breeze, she looked like some ethereal beauty born of the flowers themselves.

For a long second he squeezed his eyes shut, and when he opened them, she'd moved, walking around the flower bed onto a path that traced a circuitous route to the front gate. As she walked toward him, Zane filled his empty lungs with fragrant air and told himself he'd been hallucinating.

Julia Goodwin was no otherworldly beauty. He smiled as the strange tightness in his chest eased. It was relief, he decided, nothing more. Relief because *this* Julia Goodwin looked exactly as she should. She bore no resemblance to Friday's siren in black silk.

Good Girl Julia stopped in front of him, her smile tentative, her eyes not quite meeting his. If there'd been a street to cross, she would likely have crossed it. "I'm sorry about McCoy's welcome. He gets a bit excited around men."

"Around men, huh?" Amusement quirked the corners of Zane's mouth. "Should we go there?"

For a second she looked puzzled; then the implication of her innocent remark took hold. "Oh, no, that's not what I meant. McCoy actually belongs to my brother, and every time a man comes through that gate, he goes crazy hoping it's Mitch."

Her brother's dog—that made sense.

He'd been thinking how McCoy didn't fit the picture. Women who wore filmy dresses and whose skin looked as soft as the velvety roses overhead had lap dogs called Muffy. Or cats. Not rowdy bundles of energy such as McCoy here.

He stroked a hand over the dog's silky head. "You have a lot of men coming through your gate?"

"Visiting Kree," she replied instantly, then looked stricken. "Not in *that* way, not since she's been going out with Tagg. It's just she's so popular with guys. Ugh!" She clamped a hand over her mouth and then slowly removed it. "Do you suppose I can get my foot any further in here?"

"You could try it without the sneaker."

"Mmm, barefoot would be easier." She laughed and shook her head, and Zane remembered the laughter and the bare feet and the heat from Friday night. Then, still laughing, she looked right into his eyes, and he only remembered the heat.

Instant, blazing, intense.

About a millisecond before he went up in smoke, she blinked and looked away. Then she stooped to pet the dog and started talking—started and didn't stop talking—about needing to keep the dog chained during the day because he'd found a spot in the fence he could jump over, about how much exercise he needed after such confinement and how she'd been about to take him down by the river.

"Some days I let him run free, other days we just walk." Her monologue concluded as she straightened and smoothed an imaginary crease from her dress, and Zane noticed the leash attached to the dog's collar.

With a twinge of irritation he also noticed how she avoided looking at him, even though he was blocking the exit she obviously intended taking. He planted his feet a little wider on the path and folded his arms across his chest.

Frowning, she checked her watch. "Kree's not home yet. Thursday is her late night."

"I know. I had lunch with her today." And every day since Monday, plus a couple of dinners. Seeing as he'd been meeting her at her shop, he pretty much had Kree's routine down pat.

"Oh. You're welcome to wait for her inside."

"You trust me in your house while you're gone?"

"Why wouldn't I?" Her gaze—warm, hazel and a little perplexed—came to rest on his. "You're Kree's brother."

Trust by association. Of course. Why had he thought it might be something personal? She didn't know him. She couldn't even hold his gaze for more than a second. And the way she kept shifting her weight from one sneaker to the other—hell, she looked as if she would be more comfortable in a snake pit.

He should tell her he wasn't here for Kree. He should hand over the keys, leave, go. Hadn't he found what he'd come here to find? The real Julia? The naive good girl?

Funny, but he didn't feel reassured…or much like leaving. Call him perverse, but if she needed to go walk her dog, if she wanted him to step aside and let her by, then she could tell him straight-out instead of pussyfooting around.

Settling one hip against the gatepost, he looked around as if studying his surroundings for the first time. "You've done a great job here."

She thanked him, politely but reservedly, as if she thought his words were empty rhetoric.

That only ticked him off more, and he found himself adding, "Yeah, I like it. But if old man Plummer were still alive, he'd come after you with his shotgun."

Her eyes narrowed a fraction. "What do you mean?"

"You cut down his hedge."

"It was overgrown, and it blocked the view."

"He treasured his privacy."

"Privacy!" She made an indignant huffing sound. "I needed a chainsaw and a blowtorch to get through the wretched thing."

"That hedge was something else."

"Old man Plummer was something else." But she couldn't help the small fond smile that came with memories of the irascible recluse. "*And* he was a lousy gardener. About the only thing I kept was the cedar tree out back."

"In the northern corner?"

"Yes. Why do you ask?"

"I hung a tire swing from it one summer." He grinned, remembering. "That's one great tree."

Julia shook her head. A funny mix of surprise and wonder and delight bubbled around inside her. Not to mention the effect of that grin. *Mama mia.* She shook her head again. "I won't ask how you got past the hedge and the shotgun."

"You don't want to know." Their gazes met, held. Heat, yes, but this time it was the solid companionable warmth of a shared memory, and she didn't need to look away, to escape. This time she smiled and said, "You want to come take a look at your tree?"

He looked surprised; then the corners of his mouth curled into that killer grin. "Yeah. I'd like that."

Julia turned away quickly. The way her heart started hammering away in her chest every time he grinned might just be noticeable to a man with such an intensely sharp gaze. That grin was one the first things she'd noticed when she'd come upon him in her garden.

One of the first, right after the immediate impact of his presence.

Today the T-shirt was black, the jeans faded by work
and wash, and as he'd stooped to pat McCoy, both had
molded the hard contours of his body in a way that
screamed m-a-n. All that potent masculinity was thrown
into perfect counterbalance by the gentle frame of her pas-
tel-pink David Austen roses...the ones she'd planted to
replace old man Plummer's infamous hedge.

"I didn't know you were so familiar with this place,"
she said over her shoulder.

"We lived around the block, on Docker Street."

"I remember."

"Yeah?"

"Kree lived there, too."

"I don't recall you visiting." They came to a halt on
the open stretch of lawn behind the house, but she knew
Zane wasn't looking at the tree. As she bent to free Mac,
she felt the full force of his gaze on her.

"I wonder why that is?" he asked.

"Why do you think?"

"Scared of big brother?"

Lifting her chin, she met the intense stillness of his gaze.
"Terrified. But that's not the reason. Kree didn't ever invite me."

A touch of bitterness sharpened his silver-grey gaze and
hardened the line of his mouth. His tension seemed to
reach out and enfold her, blotting the late evening sounds
until all she could hear was the heavy pounding of her
heart. She felt sure he would say something, something to
challenge why she'd never visited her friend, something
that included the word *slumming*.

But whatever burned so harshly in his eyes remained
unsaid. He turned and walked away, stopping in front of
the tree, hands on hips, to inspect the tire she had slung
from the lowest branch.

Moving closer, he reached up and took a firm grip of the rope, as if to test its strength. The action called Julia's gaze to the width of his shoulders, to the richly tanned curve of his biceps, and she was back in that moment when she'd first seen him in her garden. Giddy, dry-mouthed, determined not to keep staring in case she hyperventilated.

Needing a distraction—*badly*—she threw a stick for Mac and watched him execute a spectacular catch. She sensed Zane's soft-footed approach, felt it in the heightened sensitivity of her skin. She rubbed her hands along her arms, but the tingling remained.

"How long is he staying?"

"Indefinitely." She tossed the stick again. "Mitch used to have a house with a yard and plenty of space, but when he got married, they moved into an apartment and he couldn't keep Mac."

"Isn't that meant to work the opposite way? Apartment first, house and yard second?"

"Oh, there's nothing usual about Mitch's marriage," Julia said without thinking. Chastened, she bit her lip. "That didn't come out right. They both travel an awful lot, so it wasn't practical to have a pet or a garden that would need care."

He didn't comment, but he looked around, taking in the rest of her yard—Mac's kennel, her well-tended herb and vegetable plot, the swing and sandpit over by the fence. She sensed a strange tension in him as he took it all in, as he turned to look at her. "Kree told me you'd been married. She didn't mention kids."

Kids? It took a second for his meaning to gel. The swing, the sandpit, the discarded toy dump truck. "Oh, no, I don't have children. These are for Joshua, for when he stays."

"Joshua?"

"Mitch and Annabel's son."

"They farm him out, too?"

He might not have been passing judgement—neither his casual tone nor his closed expression gave anything away—yet Julia's protective instincts shot to full alert. "It's only occasionally that they're both away at the same time, and I don't mind having him."

In fact, she loved having Joshua stay, loved indulging him with the simple things he missed out on, such as homemade swings and sandpits, and playing with a dog. Staying here was good for him. It wasn't *farming out*.

Feeling unduly aggrieved, she put her whole shoulder behind the next throw, then watched Mac disappear around the side of the house in frantic pursuit.

"Where is he getting out? Your fences look good."

"Around the front. It's simply not high enough."

With one of those noncommittal grunts peculiar to men, he ambled over to the side fence, studied it this way and that, then started pacing the distance between fence and house.

"It's three point six meters each side," she said, way too snappily. "And I know that by fencing it off I can enclose the backyard to keep him in. I'm saving to do it."

"What about the dog's owner? Shouldn't he be the one saving?"

"I don't think that's any concern of yours."

"You're right." He gave her a hard, sidelong look. "And it shouldn't be any concern of yours, either."

"It's my fence and my house, so that makes it my concern."

End of debate. End of yard tour. End of short nerveracking interlude with Zane O'Sullivan.

She whistled to Mac, then started for the front yard.

"Hang on a second."

He put out his arm, presumably to prevent her passing, and she walked right into it, waist height. For the life of her, she couldn't back away. She couldn't move. All she could think was *His arm, hard against my body.*

The thought caused her mouth to turn dry. Or perhaps that was because he was standing so close and making no attempt to increase the distance. Her senses were flooded with his proximity, with the absolute stillness of their bodies. It seemed as if neither of them had taken a breath in a very long while.

Then, just when she thought she might explode from the pressure, the expectancy, the not knowing what would come next or what she wanted to come next, he moved his arm…not abruptly, but in a long, slow, brushing caress across her abdomen.

She knew the instant he detected the belly button ring. She could tell by the jerk of his head, by his swift intake of breath, by the sudden tension that stiffened his whole body.

And by the look of astonishment on his face.

In another place and time that look might have been comical, but not here and now. For he still stood way too close—so close she could feel the heat emanating from his big body, and where he had touched her, oh, there was more than heat.

There was fire.

She closed her eyes, imagined his broad, long-fingered hand spread across the bare skin of her belly, swore she could feel the touch of his thumb as it circled the delicate piece of jewelry, as it slid slowly lower. A responsive flush seemed to light her skin from the inside out.

"You have a piercing?"

Julia blinked her way out of the sensual heat haze and felt his gaze skim in a quicksilver motion from her face to her belly. She swallowed, moistened her arid mouth, although she hadn't a clue what to say other than a simple, "Yes."

Should she explain how she'd felt the day after she'd signed her divorce papers? Could she explain the surge of restlessness, of recklessness, of unreality? How she had decided that was the day to do something un-Julia-like, something to mark the start of her new life. Something like getting a tattoo.

Except once she walked through the door of Skin Pix, the old Julia wouldn't stay silent. *She* didn't want the statement of a multihued butterfly stamped into her skin. She wanted something a little less obvious.

And so she had walked out the door with a silver ring in her navel.

Of course the new Julia wasn't any different to the old one. She could never bring herself to wear clothes that bared her midriff and showed off the adornment, just as she could never explain to anyone else why she'd had it done, or why she kept wearing the unseen ring.

"It's just something I did on a whim." She shrugged self-consciously. "I had better get moving. Make yourself at home—Kree shouldn't be long."

"I'm not here to see Kree."

He was still standing too close, still blocking her path, still making her feel incredibly hot and bothered. Seeking relief, she looked down…just as he slid a hand into the front pocket of his jeans. Oh, dear Lord, she should not be looking there.

"I brought your car."

Her gaze sped guiltily back to where a set of car keys now dangled from his fingers. That was what she *should* have been noticing in the front of his jeans, instead of other, um, things.

"I guess that means I owe you two drinks," she said.

His pause was infinitesimal, just long enough for Julia to notice how the levity in her tone had done nothing to ease the heavily charged atmosphere. Then, in a slow, measured tone, he said, "I thought we agreed that wasn't a good idea."

"*You* said it wasn't a good idea."

"You had a man waiting at your gate."

"I didn't invite him." Her gaze held his without wavering—an amazing feat, considering the anticipatory quiver running from her toes to the tips of her ears. "And when he rang today and asked me out to dinner, I declined."

"So?"

Julia moistened her mouth, felt the lick of his gaze follow the movement. "So what if I want to buy you those drinks?"

"You know where to find me."

"The Lion?"

"Back bar." One corner of his mouth quirked. "But we both know Julia Goodwin wouldn't be seen dead in a dive like that."

And before she could even think of a reply, let alone voice it, he pressed the car keys into her hand and sauntered off.

Three

Julia wished *she* had been the one to deliver the clever exit line and saunter off. She wished *he* had been the one left standing nonplussed in her garden. Except that scenario wasn't ever likely to happen, seeing as it completely contravened nature. Mitch had snaffled all the family genes for saber-sharp one-liners, and Chantal had garnered most of the clever DNA.

Besides, walking away would have been impolite, and Julia was always polite.

That didn't stop her wishing...or trying to devise the perfect comeback. By the time she finished walking Mac, she had declared the latter an impossibility. How could she come up with anything sassy enough to top his reaction to her piercing?

She pictured him standing in the dappled garden light, those silvery eyes dazed, his expression dumbfounded, and her body almost buzzed with the unfamiliar blend of power and pleasure. Because nice, polite Julia Goodwin had shocked—nay, *stunned*—the baddest boy ever to swagger through the corridors of Plenty High. It was an intoxicating notion, and it made her feel strong in the most female of ways.

Strong enough to walk into the Lion, to sit down beside him, to order those drinks? Probably not. But that didn't stop her enjoying the fantasy. Not even the sight of Mrs. Hertzig, patiently waiting to ambush the next passerby, could dampen the moment.

"Hello, dear. Been out walking the dog, I see."

Julia's fantasy dissolved as her elderly neighbour leaned over her front fence, eager to natter.

"We've been all the way out to Maisie's and back," Julia supplied. When Mrs. H. didn't immediately pitch a question about her best-friend-slash-rival's garden, Julia knew there was something on her mind. And as Kree liked to point out, Mrs. H. never kept anything on her mind for long. She always aired it for public consumption.

"I couldn't help noticing you had company earlier." Her lips pursed on the word *company,* giving Julia enough time to think, *Uh-oh.* "If I'm not mistaken, it was that wild O'Sullivan boy."

Boy? Julia didn't think that tag quite fit her visitor, unless defined by the word *bad.*

"Back in town to visit with his sister, is he?"

"Yes, and—"

"He's a bad egg, that one. Do you think it's wise to have him in your yard, dear? I doubt your parents would approve. Your mother won't have forgotten that window he broke in her office."

"He's grown up since then," Julia pointed out, but Mrs. H. was in full flight.

Graffiti, vandalism, theft, arson—in her mind all

Plenty's crime of the past twenty years could be laid at the feet of "That wild O'Sullivan boy." It was really too much, even for Mrs. H.

"Mrs. Hertzig? Mrs. Hertzig!" she tried a little more firmly. "Zane didn't even live in Plenty when Larbett's was broken into."

"He can drive, can't he?" And she was off again.

Julia frowned, disturbed by a side of Plenty gossip she had never considered. Then she heard the faint burr of a ringing phone.

"Excuse me, Mrs. Hertzig, but that sounds like my telephone. I'd best run and see if I can catch it."

She felt Mrs. H.'s affronted glare boring into her back as she trotted off but couldn't summon any guilt. Not even for denying her neighbour one of her few pleasures—someone to talk to, or at least to listen to her.

As Kree would likely be home by now, and if not the answering machine would pick up, there was no need to chase after the ringing phone. Except she did not want to hear any more stories about Zane's wild youth, especially those she knew had been stretched and embellished until they bore no resemblance to the truth.

As she stepped onto the veranda, the phone stopped mid-ring. She opened the front door and called, "If that's for me, I'm home."

Kree's head—an extraordinary shade of strawberry-blonde this week—appeared from the living room doorway. "Chantal," she mouthed.

Since Julia's dinner party no-show, her sister had been very cool. She would turn even frostier when she found out Julia had passed on dating Dan.

"I'll take Mac," Kree offered as she handed the receiver over; then she winked cheekily. "Don't say anything I wouldn't say."

Which left plenty of leeway. Julia settled into the nearest armchair and put the receiver to her ear. "Hello, sis. What's new?"

She hadn't moved when Kree returned sometime later. "That dog is such a guy. You know what he—" She came to an abrupt halt when she saw Julia's face. "Hey, what's up? Is it your parents? Has there been an accident?"

"No. It's nothing like that." Julia's attempt at a reassuring smile failed badly, so she focused on the pattern in her Axminster rug as she struggled to put the crux of the phone call into words. "You know Paul's cousin-in-law who works at Chantal's law firm?"

"Janet Harrington?"

"She told Chantal that Paul is having a baby."

"Wow." Kree raked both hands through her short spiky hair. "How did that happen!"

"In the usual fashion, I should expect."

Kree didn't laugh at her attempted humor, but then it wasn't a particularly funny attempt. Instead her eyes clouded with concern as she peered into Julia's face. "How do you feel about it?"

"I'm still working on that one. I mean, how should I feel? He's not my husband anymore. He has a new wife and obviously they've decided to start a family."

"Doesn't mean you can't feel something."

"Okay, so maybe I feel a little… I don't know…"

"Heck, Jules, you were married to the schmuck for six years and he didn't give you a thing worth keeping. She's married to him six minutes and she gets a baby. You've a right to feel cheated."

Cheated. Did that describe how she felt? Did it explain the strange sense of hollowness, the emotional black hole where her reaction should reside? Perhaps she should feel cheated by her seeming lack of emotion. Something more palpable, like the sharp spike of jealousy or the bitter taste of regret, would make more sense.

A baby was the one thing she had wanted, desperately, from her marriage, but Paul had wanted to wait a few more years. Paul had insisted they wait. And now she was fast approaching thirty, with no prospect of ever experiencing the joy of carrying a baby, of childbirth and motherhood.

"What if I can't have one, Kree? What if I never do?"

Her voice sounded as empty as she felt, but there must have been something in her eyes, a trace of pain or the hint of a plea, because Kree sank down onto the arm of her chair.

"Oh, honey, there's no need to think like that, not when you've never even tried."

"By the time I do try, my ovaries will be all shriveled up."

"Probably." But there was compassion in her smile, and in her spontaneous hug. "But, hey, why do you need a baby? You have me to look after, and God knows I can be pretty immature."

Julia couldn't help but smile.

"And if you think *not* having a baby's tragic, imagine if you *had* had one with Paul Petulant. What if the kid was just like daddy? Can you picture a two-year-old version of your ex-husband? The tantrums?" Kree gave a melodramatic shudder. "Honestly, Jules, you did not want that man's child!"

She squeezed a little tighter before letting go and springing to her feet. Sitting still was not in Kree's nature. Nor was dwelling on an issue.

"Enough of the sappy stuff—I feel like a drink. You gonna join me?"

"I don't think so."

"Come on," she cajoled. "Let's mix up something exotic, and then we can discuss your sex life."

Julia rolled her eyes.

"Oh, that's right. You don't *have* a sex life, a small matter which will need remedying if you're ever going to have that baby you yearn for."

"I'm not about to go out and pick someone up just to get pregnant, if that's what you're implying. You know that's not what I want."

"Yeah, I know. All I'm saying is how do you expect to find this prince you so desperately want to marry and make babies with, when you spend half your life sitting around here? You need to get out more, have some fun, kiss a few frogs."

"I've been meeting plenty of frogs." *I just haven't been kissing any of them.*

"Yes, well, your sister does seem to know her fair share."

With the mood successfully lightened, Kree leaned down and tweaked Julia's ponytail. "If you won't try a new cocktail, how about trying a new colour?"

Julia started to shake her head.

"Oh, come on, Jules, this is exactly what you need. I could do you tomorrow after work. A decent cut, some red highlights—you'd be a new woman by nightfall."

It wasn't the first time Kree had begged to be let loose on Julia's hair, but it was the first time Julia had been tempted. *A new woman by nightfall.* She liked the sound of that.

Sensing capitulation, Kree danced around the chair, talking colours and styles. All excited animation, she dragged her fingers through her own hair, and the spikes stood up like the Opera House sails. Julia shook her head firmly. What was she thinking?

"I'm sorry, Kree, but I like my hair the way it is."

Kree studied her for a long, silent moment, her blue gaze uncharacteristically somber. "Yes, but do you like your life the way it is?"

"I don't know," Julia admitted honestly.

"Then I'll keep that appointment free."

Kree's question hammered at Julia that night and right through the next day at work. There were aspects of her life she treasured. Her home, for one, and her close relationship with her family. Her many friendships, her standing in the community.

But if she were truly content, she wouldn't have lain awake half the night mulling over other aspects of her life. She wouldn't be accepting blind dates in the hope of finding another husband. She wouldn't feel this yawning hollowness whenever she thought of her future without said husband and family. And she definitely wouldn't be dwelling on the fantasy of being a new woman by nightfall. The last time she'd started thinking that way, she'd ended up with her navel pierced.

And was that a bad thing? Did she want to wear the label of Good Girl forever? Or did she want the stimulating buzz that came from shocking the unshockable?

If only she could find answers as easily as she found questions. By the time the store closed and she started dragging her feet home, Julia was no closer to those answers. As she neared Bill's garage, her feet picked up their pace in time with her pulse, and it took a huge effort of willpower to prevent her gaze from raking the drive-through or peering into the yawning entrance to the workshop.

She could have saved herself the effort.

He wasn't in the garage; he was in the street outside, talking to the driver of a flashy red car. Her surprise at finding him there brought her to a dead stop in the middle of the footpath.

Time seemed to hit that same brick wall as she took in his casual posture, one hand splayed on the roof, the other tapping a beat on the driver's door. As usual, his hair picked up the glow of the sun and threw it back tenfold. As usual, her gaze caught on the hard outline of his arms, bared by a sleeveless black shirt. As usual, he looked so arresting, so vital, so male, that it took several of those long, slow-motion moments before anything else registered.

The *anything else* brought real time back with a sickening crash. The driver he seemed so cosy with was a woman…a woman who looked as fast and flashy as her car. A woman such as that wouldn't have compromised on the tattoo. She wouldn't hesitate about walking into a bar and buying a man a drink, especially a man who looked like Zane O'Sullivan.

Something fired deep in Julia's stomach, something she didn't wait to analyze but which cried *New woman by nightfall* as she turned on her heel, then kept up the chant all the way back to the main shopping center.

When she walked into Hair Today and selected a chair, Kree's eyes boggled. "Tell me I'm hallucinating."

"You are not to come anywhere near me with scissors," Julia replied sternly. "And if you insist on red, fine, but only highlights. If you make it as red as Alice Pratt's, then you will need to find another place to live."

Kree did insist on red, and Julia was glad. She studied her reflection in her bathroom mirror for about the twentieth time and shook her head in that deliberate measured way of hair product models. She was getting quite good at it, she decided as her blunt-cut layers swung in a wide arc before settling on her shoulders.

And she laughed out loud, at first because she couldn't help herself—the delight just uncoiled like an overwound spring set loose—and then in recollection of Kree revealing the colour. Paprika.

Julia had flown out of the chair, her eyes wide with horror. "That sounds like orange."

"No," Kree said as she eased her back down. "That sounds like hot."

Did she look hot? Julia narrowed her eyes to inspect her image more objectively. The woman staring back at her didn't look like Julia Goodwin. She looked like… Julia tried a pout. Oh, my, she thought with a wild fluttering of excitement in the pit of her stomach. She could almost pass for one of those models. She could pass for a woman who drove a red sports car.

"And what are you going to do about it?" Kree had asked when she saw the fascinated look on her friend's face. Then she'd nudged her with a friendly elbow. "You gonna take your new look frog-hunting?"

They'd laughed uproariously over that. Then Kree tried to talk her into going night-clubbing in Cliffton with her and Tagg. Julia refused, although she didn't share her reason. Her stomach jittered again, then settled.

Now all she had to do was decide what one wore to a place like the Lion. She started by taking a deep breath and doing something she had never done in her life, something ill-mannered and borderline illicit. She opened the vanity drawer where Kree kept her considerable stash of cosmetics and toiletries, and helped herself.

*   *   *

Zane glared at his king-size bourbon as if it were the cause of his king-size case of moodiness. He knew it wasn't the drink's fault, but that didn't stop him staring it down. Nor was it the fault of his neighbour at the bar, although that hadn't stopped him shredding the bloke when he tried to pass the time of day. Shoulders hunched, he glared past his drink and noticed the bartender veer wider as he passed, eyeing him much the same way as he would a savage dog.

Wise man, Zane thought with a mental snarl.

He was out of sorts because he didn't want to be here, not here in this bar, and especially not here in Plenty. No matter how much time passed, the town never changed, nor did his response. He'd driven past the old grain silos at the edge of town and he was eleven years old again…or thirteen, or fifteen. It didn't matter which. He was an intruder, an object of suspicion and unwanted charity, stuck in a place where he could never belong.

He looked around the Lion again, then shook his head with disgust. Who the hell was he looking for, anyhow? The only person he wanted to see walk through the door would be home in her doll's cottage doing needlework or arranging flowers or entertaining men who drove Volvos. Forget that he'd deliberately baited her about coming down here. That wasn't going to happen.

He could just go around and pound on her pretty blue door and demand some answers to all the questions chasing their tails around his brain. Questions about why she'd bought a house on the poor side of town, why she couldn't afford to dog-proof the fence, and why she had that piercing. Questions about what other anomalies lay behind her Good Girl image.

Except that wasn't going to happen, either.

Not when the only thing likely to improve his mood

wasn't answers to questions he had no right asking but sex, hot and uncomplicated sex. Maybe he would stand a chance if he stopped snarling at every female who looked his way—and there had been a few since trade hotted up in the last hour.

Maybe later. Maybe if he could force this drink down.

The perfume reached him first, a scent so strong it rode roughshod over the thick smoke-and-beer aroma of the bar. He recognized the perfume and placed its owner instantly. Big hair, medium sports coupe, small carburettor problem.

"Well, hi there, you."

She insinuated herself between his stool and the next, so close that her scantily clad flesh pressed against his arm and his thigh. His whole body recoiled.

"Aren't you going to say hello?" she cooed.

At the garage this afternoon he'd played along in the name of customer relations, but now he was on his own time. He didn't have to play nice. He figured a curt "No" would get the message across, but she laughed and wriggled even closer.

"You were so helpful with my little car trouble today. Can I buy you a drink?"

Couldn't she see the full glass in his hand? Maybe all that gunk she wore on her eyes impaired her vision.

"I'm not thirsty."

Five red-tipped fingers tiptoed across his shoulder, and he swore his skin crawled. "Maybe you'd rather dance? This is a hot band."

"I don't dance," he growled through his teeth.

"Hey, Prudence, you trying to chase away my customers?" the barman called from down the bar.

Prudence. Zane shook his head at the irony of her name. Didn't that just beat everything? But at least she stomped off, after letting him know with a few choice words what he was missing. He didn't figure he would lose any sleep over it.

Obviously he'd been wrong about what he needed to improve his mood. He could sit there all night and drink bourbon until it seeped out his ears, and he still wouldn't be interested in what Prudence offered. And before he started thinking about what kind of woman he *did* want that hot, uncomplicated sex with, he would drag his miserable hide out of there.

He downed his drink in one swallow and flattened his hands on the bar as the liquor kicked home hard. When his vision cleared, he was looking straight into the mirror over the bar. Which was when he saw Julia come through the door.

Three things registered simultaneously. She was wearing a black dress. She had done something with her hair. He wasn't going anywhere.

Her head turned slowly, as if she were scanning the packed room, searching for someone. The instant she saw him, he knew that someone was him. His whole body quickened with the knowledge as she started toward him, zigzagging through the crowd with a single-minded look on her face. She disappeared entirely behind a huge block of a guy in a red plaid shirt, and tension grabbed hold of his throat. When she reappeared, laughing at something the big guy had said, he relaxed. Marginally.

She looked up then, straight into the mirror, and when she saw him watching, she smiled. That smile slugged him right in the chest. He might have smiled right back—*should* have smiled right back—but with every muscle in his body feeling as tight as a machine-wound locknut, that was impossible. He watched her walk the last ten feet and stop beside him.

"About time," he said shortly.

She blinked, her smile fading, but she kept her eyes focused on his. In the mirror. ''What are you drinking?''

''Bourbon.''

''And?''

''More bourbon.''

She edged into the narrow gap between the stools and leaned forward to look across the bar. While she tried to catch the barman's eye, Zane took the opportunity to look at her, to try to discern why his body reacted so extravagantly to the sight of her.

He noticed that her black dress was actually a skirt and top. Compared with this place's usual skimpy dress, it was pretty tame. Nothing for a man's libido to get in a lather over. His eyes noted how her skirt skimmed her hips—a neat fit, not too tight—before flaring to a modest mid-calf length. Of course his libido discerned the faint line of high-cut underwear where it skimmed her hips and immediately started lathering.

Disgusted with his response, he forced his gaze upward to her sleeveless shirt. Seeing as it had little flowers all over, it was probably called something prissy, like a blouse. There was nothing sexy about a blouse. Then she leaned a little further across the bar, and the hem rode up enough to bare a thin sliver of smooth skin.

Maybe he'd been too long out west, too long only seeing skin as sun-wizened as the harsh Pilbara landscape, but the sight of her soft, milk-pale skin took him way past lathering. He practically howled.

He looked up and found her watching him. She knew exactly what he had been examining—he saw the knowledge in her eyes, in the tinge of colour along the side of her slender neck, in the slightly stiff smile she offered. ''The barman doesn't seem to want to come down this end.''

"That's because I scared him away."

The last three-quarters of his sentence was drowned out when the band started up again, louder than ever, after a break. Julia shrugged and leaned closer. "I didn't catch that."

She pulled back, but not all the way, obviously waiting for him to repeat himself. Into her ear. His mouth went dry thinking about it. Slowly, he leaned toward her, and she bent, giving him open access to her ear and her neck. *Her soft, smooth, dawn-scented neck.* He swallowed, lifted a hand and pushed back the thick fall of her hair, tucking it behind her ear. It was his only excuse for touching its rich texture, and it felt as silky as it looked.

Only then did he remember why she'd allowed him so near. "The barman—I scared him away."

She nodded, and they both eased back. But he knew in that instant that she was registering the same things, remembering the same details. The way their arms had touched, skin to skin, heat to heat. How her skirt had brushed against his thighs, how the filmy material clung as she'd eased away.

A faint flush tinged her exposed ear as she searched out the barman again. Without her contact, Zane felt deprived. He didn't want a drink. He wanted her close, those thighs against his, his hands in her hair, his mouth against her neck.

He grabbed her by the hand and pulled her back against him. Her eyes rounded in surprise and for a second he was sidetracked by their amazing blend of green and grey and rich warm brown. Then he lifted a handful of hair from her neck, wrapped it 'round his fingers and leaned in close.

Knowing it wasn't an honest way to get close to her, knowing it had nothing to do with moving to the rhythm and everything to do with body contact, didn't stop him.

"Forget the drink," he growled. "Let's dance."

Four

Julia loved to dance.

At home, in private, she often shook her *groove thang* to something upbeat from Kree's CD collection. Sometimes, if she knew Mrs. H. was out, she would turn up the volume until the pastel walls of Honeysuckle Cottage vibrated with the bass beat.

Or perhaps they simply quaked with horror. She was pretty certain Ben Plummer's musical taste hadn't stretched to hip-hop.

So when Zane had growled, "Let's dance," she'd raised no objections...not that he'd given her any option.

As he pulled her toward the dance floor in the adjoining room, her heart raced. She could have blamed the exertion of keeping up with his long strides, but she didn't.

Her heart raced with excitement, with eagerness and exhilaration. Oh, she wanted to dance, all right. She wanted to wiggle her hips and shimmy her butt. She wanted to snake her arms in those slinky moves Kree had taught her one margarita-imbued girls-night-in. She wanted to swing her head until her sexy new hair caught fire in the strobing lights.

She wanted to dance until she'd forgotten all about women in red cars, all about kissing frogs, and especially all about Paul and babies and empty hollow places that might never be filled.

The band launched into a raunchy rock anthem as Zane pulled her onto the packed floor. The pounding beat kept time with her pulse, reverberated through her blood and coaxed her body into motion. She swung her head, felt her hair soar in a wide floating arc, and she laughed out loud with delight.

Laughed and gyrated and snaked her arms. Through a heavy veil of tumbled hair she saw Zane watching her, the look on his face almost as bemused as when he'd discovered her piercing. Bemused and empowering. This was exactly what she needed. She laughed again, and he closed the gap between them, leaning close when she stopped jumping around. He lifted her hair as he had done in the bar.

When his fingers grazed the side of her neck, Julia shivered, not with cold but with sudden heat.

The music, the press of the crowd, her own heightened state of self-awareness, all receded into some other dimension as her senses filled with his nearness, his scent, the pressure of those callous-tipped fingers as they slid around her nape, holding her still. The dip of his head as he leaned into her ear.

''What's so funny?''

His breath swirled against her skin; his thumb feathered across her earlobe. And an out-of-control dancer crashed into her, propelling her forward.

Hard up against Zane.

For a long while she didn't think to breathe—she *couldn't* think. Full stop. Her head spun with sensation. Thighs pressed flush against his thighs, her breasts flattened against the solid wall of his chest, his hands firm on her shoulders, steadying her. Her hands at his hard-muscled waist, right where his soft cotton shirt tucked into snug-fitting jeans.

And everywhere they touched, heat. Incredible, bone-melting heat.

She took a long ragged breath, but instead of oxygen her lungs filled with the scent of clean shirt and hot man. Longing, pure and elemental, flooded her senses. She wanted to wrap her arms around his hard body, to burrow her nose into that soft shirt. She wanted time to savor the intense pleasure of man-woman contact.

As if party to her thoughts, his body tensed beneath her hands, and she knew he was about to set her back in her own dancing space. Disappointment settled as heavily as the crashing denouement to the band's current number. He backed up enough for hands to slide away, enough for eyes to meet and hold. The song ended with a flurry of drums and cymbals, leaving a silence as thick as the preceding noise, as intense as his unfathomable gaze.

"You didn't say what you were laughing about."

"Oh, just me. Dancing. It's not something I do often." With a sweeping gesture, she indicated the room at large. "Not like this."

"I told you this place wasn't your style."

That wasn't what she'd meant, at least not in the way he'd obviously interpreted it. But before she could explain, the strobing lights cut out, leaving the glow from one slowly spinning orb to illuminate the floor. A lone guitar struck the opening chords to the next song.

A ballad....

Couples shuffled into slow-dancing clinches, singles shuffled back to the bar, and Julia's pulse shuffled into a quick-step beat. It was way out of time with the slow torchy song. She felt Zane's hand at her back, firmly guiding her forward, ushering her from the floor.

No. She stopped so suddenly, turned so quickly, that he almost bumped into her. She couldn't look at him, not into that hard, closed expression, not when she was about to tell a small fib. So she focused on his chest, on the top button of his shirt, and crossed the fingers of both hands. "This is more my style."

"You want to dance to *this?*" he asked slowly.

"Yes."

It took forever, that moment of total immobility, of not even breathing, of silent pleading. *Dance with me, Zane. Please don't walk away.* All that moved, eventually, were a few strands of her hair, stirred by his heavy exhalation. As if he, too, had been holding his breath.

He muttered something low and rough, but to Julia it sounded like a good answer. Especially when she felt his hands on her shoulders, moving down her back, pulling her right in close to his body. When she felt the touch of his thighs as he started to dance, she let *her* hands slide up his chest and loop around his neck, and released her own backed-up breath in a long, slow, sigh of relief.

Thank you, God.

With a small, satisfied smile, she rested her cheek against his chest and settled into the slow sway. It had been two years since her divorce, three since Paul had left her, much longer since she had been this close to a man. It shouldn't have felt so instantly right, so intensely good. There should have been a few minutes of awkwardness, of trodden toes and bumped knees, but they seemed to adjust instinctively, to fit perfectly.

Eyes closed, she hummed along to the song, one she'd never particularly liked but now wished would never end. When the lyrics implored her to hold on tight, she tangled her fingers in the ends of his hair and obeyed. And when the third in the series of slow numbers ended, she didn't want to let go. She might never have let go if Zane hadn't done the job for her.

Slowly she blinked her eyes back into focus and her mind back into reality.

People were leaving the floor, some edging around them and a nearby couple. Completely oblivious, *they* remained locked from knee to chest...and mouth to mouth. Julia felt a betraying heat in her ears, her neck, the pit of her stomach. She felt Zane watching, reading her face with his sharp silver gaze, knowing.

She wanted to be kissed. As thoroughly as that other girl. By him.

And when his gaze slid to her mouth, she knew he wanted it, too. Her pulse thundered as she watched his hand lift, reach for her, then check. The backs of his fingers brushed against her cheek, and delicious shivers of sensation rioted through her body.

"You want to get out of here?"

In a heartbeat.

But before she could reply, voices intruded, one of them coming into clear focus when it repeated her name.

"*Julia?* It *is* you! I said it was, but Kerrie said no, not here. Not in this bar. Who'd have thought it?"

Obviously not Mel McLaren and Kerrie Hall. Julia acknowledged her workmates with a wan smile. Not that they noticed—both were too busy gaping at Zane. Hadn't their mothers taught them it was rude to stare?

Engrossed eyes still locked on Zane, Mel continued. "We've all got a big table over by the stage. You wanna join us?"

Julia cleared her throat. "We had a spot at the bar—"

"Which undoubtedly disappeared two seconds after your butt left the seat," Kerrie interjected. "The ole Cat hasn't seen a crowd like this since the millennium bash."

"So, how 'bout it?" Mel persisted.

Judging by Zane's closed expression, it was her call. She bit her lip. If she admitted she was about to leave with Zane O'Sullivan, all of Gracey's would know by nine-o-five tomorrow morning, all of Plenty a few hours later. But she did want to leave with him—now, before she lost her nerve.

"I wasn't staying long," she prevaricated, while her eyes appealed to Zane for help.

"Count me out," he said shortly. "Thanks for the dance."

He turned on his heel and walked away, leaving Julia the focus of inquisitive attention.

"You got to rub bellies with Bad-ass O'Sullivan? *Hubba-hubba!*"

"Thanks a bunch for the introduction, *mate!*"

Mel sounded awed, Kerrie peeved. And for once Julia didn't much care what anyone thought. She stood there watching *Bad-ass* O'Sullivan walk away without a by-your-leave and she felt…cheated.

Yes, cheated. This time the description really did fit. She hadn't gone to all this trouble just to be abandoned after five minutes on the dance floor.

So when Mel linked arms with her, imploring her to, "Come and join the dots, you dark horse," she carefully but politely reclaimed her arm.

"I'm sorry but I can't stay. I'm on early shift tomorrow."

At first she thought she'd lost him—those long-striding legs had carried him out the side door with astonishing speed—but then she caught a glimpse of movement on the outside stairs leading to the hotel's accommodation wing. A figure moved from dark shadow into a pool of light on the second-story landing, and surprise steadied the simmering irritation that had triggered Julia's chase.

Did he have a room here?

"Zane?"

Halfway up the second flight, he didn't just stop, he completely stilled.

"When you mentioned getting out of here, I thought you meant *us*, as in you and me."

She didn't raise her voice, yet it carried clear and strong across the deserted courtyard. It sounded like the voice of a woman who knew exactly what she was doing, not a woman whose stomach churned with trepidation.

She didn't hear his sigh, but his body language told her there was one. "Go back inside, Julia. Back to your friends."

"They're not my friends. We work together at Gracey's, but I never see them socially, and I certainly don't want to go and sit with them. Not when they only want to grill me about *you*."

"Huh."

Imagine that. An answer that revealed nothing except a mild derision. Julia's irritation flared anew, and she found herself crossing the courtyard to glare up at him. And, God help her, she never glared. "So far I have nothing to tell them."

"Tell them I sent you home where you belong."

His harsh dismissive tone hurt, but insinuating she had no right to be there…that just aggravated the scratchy edges of her temper. Until that minute she'd never thought she had a temper, either, but there it was, forcing her to declare, "I have as much right to be here as you or Mel or anyone else!"

Inside, the band started into its next song, and she didn't hear his answer. *If* he answered.

Frustration seethed through her blood. She hated the tricky light that disguised his reaction, hated being down there cricking her neck to look up at him, hated how she would need to raise her voice to be heard. "I'll go—if you come back down here and answer one question."

The singer warbled two full lines of a shabby old standard before Zane shrugged, muttered something indecipherable and started down the stairs. She met him at the bottom, where the reflected radiance from a nearby neon sign painted the darkness with an eerie sheen.

"Well?" He almost grunted the question, but when he tilted his head she caught the silvery glint of his eyes. Guarded, yes, but there was more. Wariness? Apprehension? She scoffed at the notion. What did *he* have to fear? She was the one with stage fright. She was the one in urgent need of a clever script, or at least enough cleverness to improvise.

"Are you staying here?"

"Yes."

"Why? I mean, I thought you'd be staying with Bill."

"Yeah, well, he always offers the invitation, but a midget wouldn't be comfortable sleeping on his couch."

She hadn't thought much about it, but the residence attached to the garage was probably one-bedroom. Ideal for a bachelor like Bill, but not for company, especially company as large as the package standing in front of her, turning as if to leave.

Without thinking, Julia lunged for him, grabbing at his arm to prevent his departure. "Where are you going?"

"Upstairs. To bed. You asked for one question, I've already answered three."

Julia felt something resembling a snarl building in her throat. "None of them was *the* question, and you know it!"

With pointed deliberation, his gaze skimmed down to where she still held on to his arm. Fiercely.

"Oh. I'm sorry." Horrified that she hadn't noticed her grip turn forceful, she let go, then rubbed her hand over his forearm, over where her nails had probably scored his skin. "I didn't realize. I really am *so* sorry."

"The question?" he asked tersely.

She sucked up a draft of bravery, crossed her fingers for luck and hoped she wasn't about to make a first-class fool of herself. "Why did you change your mind?"

"About?"

"Whatever you were thinking when you asked if I wanted to get out of there."

His gaze flicked to her mouth. She felt it tingle with awareness, felt a heavy heat settle low in her stomach.

"That wasn't my mind doing the thinking," Zane admitted. If he'd been using his brain, he wouldn't have danced with her, wouldn't have let his body decide it was in with a chance. And he sure wouldn't have felt such biting regret when her workmates happened along.

Hell, he should go shout them all a great big thank-you drink for gawking from her to him as if they were as mismatched as…as they were. Forget how perfect she felt in his arms. Forget the kiss-me message in the molten warmth of her eyes. Forget dragging her out of that crowd and—

"You haven't answered my question."

"Yeah, I did. If you didn't like my answer, tough."

"That was *not* an answer. Why can't you just talk straight to me, Zane? I'm a big girl—I can take the truth. If you're not interested, then why did you lead me on? Why did you look at me like you couldn't wait to get me somewhere private, like you couldn't wait to get your hands and your mouth on me?"

The words spilled from her tongue, tumbling one on top of the other like ball bearings from an overturned tub. And he could tell she regretted knocking that tub over. Her eyes widened; her mouth hung open a second, then compressed as tight as a zipper. So much for straight speak, Zane thought with a cynical twist of his lips. Next she'll start apologizing and biting her damn lip, and that'll really piss—

"I'm sorry. I shouldn't have said that."

"Why?" He took a step closer. "What happened to talking straight?"

Biting her lip, she took an even longer step away. That was it! Zane advanced, she retreated, until he'd crowded her against the wall, until his palms were planted against the brick wall on either side of her head.

"Is that what you want, Julia? My hands on you?"

He touched her hair, sifted it through his fingers, dragged silken handfuls up from her neck. Looked right into those amazing eyes that seemed to draw colour from her mood. Right now they shone amber with desire.

"Is that why you followed me out here?" he whispered roughly. "Because you want my mouth on you?"

The *oh-yes-please* sound low in her throat was about the sexiest thing he'd ever heard, so that was where he put his mouth. Right there on skin so pale it almost glowed in the

pearlescent light. One touch, lips against skin, and the slow
burn in his gut combusted like a gasoline fire.

Releasing her hair, he touched thumb to bottom lip,
sampling its soft moisture as he dipped his head. A whisper
away, he paused, wanting to savor the keen edge of anticipation. Needing to know he could contain the fire. An
impatient growl resonated in her throat. Then her hands
fisted in his shirt and *she* was pressing her mouth to his,
a mouth both soft with welcoming warmth and strong with
determined demands.

He opened his mouth over hers and immediately found
the perfect angle to access all that heat, all those flavors
of desire. When his tongue touched hers, he groaned and
pressed her closer to the wall, and something that felt like
a smile of deepest primitive satisfaction rose up in him,
something stronger than the physical demands that pressed
his body against hers.

Because she not only wanted this kiss, she seemed to
want it as badly as he did.

Her hands caressed his back in restless circles; his
tongue stroked across her inner lip; her leg climbed the
side of his thigh, and the hotel door immediately to their
left crashed open. Zane barely had time to register surprise—it was a rarely used exit—before a rowdy trio reeled
out into the courtyard. His groan was heartfelt, although
Julia took it as a sign of encouragement and tried to re-
claim his lips. He'd managed to peel half her fingers from
his shirt and was trying to quiet her throaty protests when
one of the drunks wavered to a halt.

"Who's there?" He peered in their direction then called
to his friend. "Hey, Jeddo, there's folks over here."

Zane presumed it was Jeddo who conjectured, crudely,
what folks might be doing in the dark, but he ground his
teeth to hold his tongue in check. Lecturing a drunk was

less than pointless, less than futile. They came closer, and Zane stepped in front of Julia, shielding her from their view.

"Who you got there, man? Somebody's missus?"

With a sinking feeling, Zane recognized his bar-stool neighbour from earlier in the night, the one he'd told to take a hike. He took only a few seconds longer to identify Zane.

"Well looky here, if it ain't Mista Congee—Mr. Congeenee—"

He broke off with a curse, and Zane shook his head. He didn't strike Zane as a man who could handle six-syllable words sober, let alone in his current condition.

"Holy—it's Julia. You know her, Jeddo, the mayor's little girl."

Hell. While he'd been concentrating on Mr. Congeniality, his mates had edged into a position to see Julia.

"What're you doin' out here, Joo-lee-ah Goodwin?"

"Shoot, Bart, ain't it obvious?"

Jeddo put the obvious into words of one syllable, and after that everything happened in a blur of fury. Zane seized him by the shirtfront and suggested he wash his mouth out. Bart attached himself, leechlike, to Zane's back. With his mates hooting encouragement, the third managed to land a glancing blow to Zane's face, and he would have returned the compliment if Julia hadn't been there.

It was enough that she'd been insulted—that he'd allowed these jerks to insult her—without starting a brawl.

What the… Zane's heart leapfrogged into his throat. Arms held wide, she had stepped in front of the guy with his fists drawn and was calmly asking if he really wanted to punch Mayor Goodwin's little girl.

"What the hell do you think you're doing?"

Almost numb with fear, he roared the words, knocked both parasites from his body in one savage motion and wrestled her out of harm's way. When he turned, all three were backing up. One of them yelled a final obscenity that had him revving to go after him.

"Later, bud."

The soft promise held more menace than he'd intended, and they scampered out of the yard and disappeared into the darkness.

Adrenaline still coursed through his body as he whirled on Julia. "You want to answer *my* question now?"

Unlike the drunks, she didn't back away from his furious countenance. She lifted her chin and faced him squarely. "I was dealing with the situation in a reasonable manner."

Zane snorted. "You can't reason with drunks. Didn't Mayor Goodwin teach you that?"

"Who says you can't?"

He jabbed a thumb at his chest. "*I* say you can't, and unlike you, I know from experience."

Her eyes narrowed a little, and Zane silently cursed himself. He didn't want her questioning him on his experience of drunks. He didn't want to go there. And he had no right yelling at her. He let go a long, fractured breath. "Come on. I'll walk you home."

"Thank you."

She started walking, her posture a little stiff, defensive. He raked a hand through his hair. "Look, I'm sorry. I shouldn't have taken my anger out on you. It wasn't your fault. I shouldn't have put you in a position where you needed to reason with drunks in the first place."

"I don't recall you dragging those idiots out here. Or me, for that matter. I made that choice, Zane."

He smiled wryly. "Bad choice, huh?"

"Not really." And she smiled back. Man, he loved that smile. It seemed to reach right over and extract the remaining dregs of his fury, to suck them right out of his body. "I had fun."

"Up until the end."

"Oh, I was pretty much enjoying myself then, too. I've never seen a barroom brawl before."

"You shouldn't have been in a position—"

"Will you stop taking responsibility for that? Please?" She looked down, then up again, a slightly abashed look on her face. "Perhaps I should apologize for attacking you the way I did."

"It was…unexpected."

"Yes, well, it kind of shocked me, as well. That's not what I would have expected myself to do, and certainly not what others would expect of me. No wonder those guys were so surprised."

"Your workmates, too."

"Why do you say that?"

"The way they stared. It was obvious they didn't expect to see you with someone like me."

Julia laughed dryly and shook her head. "They were staring because, in Mel's words, you're hubba-hubba. They didn't expect to see *you* with someone like me."

"A good girl like you?"

"I'm no bad girl, that's for sure."

"You have a piercing." He cut her a sidelong look. "And if it was just a spur-of-the-moment thing, why do you still wear the ring?"

Perceptive. Julia had known that all along, had probably known it as a teenager, when he'd unnerved her so easily. It was his watchfulness. The way he looked right into her, seeing more than she wanted to show.

"You sure you weren't trying to be a bad girl?" he teased. "Did you invite Kree to move in to tutor you?"

"We always got along. It's that yin and yang thing."

They both smiled, but Julia felt a change in the mood, a subtle shift, as if they both were contemplating the need for yin and yang to make a whole.

Or the more pragmatic option: *opposites attract.*

The screech of tires accelerating on bitumen sliced through the balmy night air, and Zane crossed behind her, positioning himself between her and the road. Julia felt a peculiar little zap of pleasure at the protective gesture. Then the car responsible sped by them, and she shook her head reproachfully.

"You know that punk?"

"Brandon Jeffreys. He's heading down the same street as his brother." She caught his quizzical glance. "You made *his* acquaintance a little while back. Little guy with a big mouth. Name of Bart."

"Plenty's own band of yobbos—who'd have thought it?"

"You think we're all model citizens?"

"There are enough who think of themselves that way to make the rest of us move on real fast."

With Mrs. H.'s condemnation still fresh in her mind, it felt wrong to disagree. Yet Julia did disagree. If he kept on moving, how could the town's Mrs. H.'s get to know him, to see that he'd outgrown his past, that he was quite the gentleman? She smiled at that.

"I'm wondering what the model citizens would make of your gentlemanly manners."

He made a scoffing sound. Then, as if he couldn't help himself, he asked, "Why do you say that?"

"Oh, the fact that when you heard that car, you shifted to get between me and the road. And the way you tried to shield me back at the hotel. And seeing me home isn't something those model citizens would expect you to do, either.''

''They'd assume I have ulterior motives.''

''The kind where you invite yourself in for coffee and we both know it's not for coffee?'' She deliberately chose a light, teasing tone, because they had arrived at her gate and her stomach felt anything but light, her mood anything but teasing.

Smile firmly in place, she turned to face him. He wasn't smiling. It was quiet but for the booming beat of her heart, and far off, perhaps at the brand-new traffic lights back on Main, the squeal of tires under heavy punishment.

He lifted his head as if listening to that sound; then he took a step back, and Julia's chest tightened with unexplainable panic. She didn't want him to walk away, didn't want the night to end here.

''So…would you like to come in? For coffee?'' She tried the teasing smile again but knew it didn't come off. It felt strained, unnatural.

''I don't drink coffee.''

''I know.''

Something flickered across the surface of his eyes like the touch of moonlight on water, but that was the only thing that moved. ''I'm leaving soon. Could be any day now.''

''I know,'' she said calmly. And despite the warm stillness of the summer night that surrounded them like a velvet cloak, a shiver skittered up her spine.

That was the point, wasn't it? The whole heady excitement of this surreal night. With Zane O'Sullivan she didn't want those other days, she only wanted *now*. For all those other days, she would choose safe and secure and responsible.

Her gaze shifted from those difficult eyes to where a lucky fist had connected with his cheekbone. "I can put something on your face, so why don't you come in anyway?"

Five

"I'll just put the kettle on, and then I'll go get what I need."

"What is it you need?"

Halfway to the kitchen, Julia stopped, took a deep breath and turned back to face him.

He stood in the entrance hall, no further into her house than when she'd closed the front door. Its powder-blue panels framed the hard lines of his big, tensely held body—his shoulders looked broad enough to span the space between her rose-sprig-papered walls. Beyond his left arm she could just make out one delicate curl of a porcelain coat hook. At this moment it looked insubstantial, incapable of supporting a muslin throw, let alone an overcoat.

Yes, he looked pretty much as she'd imagined he would that first night when he'd driven her home. Big, broad, masculine—and completely out of place.

And his unsmiling sharp-eyed intensity sent another of those stray shivers scuttling through her system. Oh, dear Lord, he'd asked what she needed, and he hadn't been referring to first-aid supplies. Back at the hotel she'd been so certain. Outside her front gate the doubt-bunny had tapped her on the shoulder, yet she'd still felt relatively sure. As for now...

Should she say she'd made a mistake? Could she simply ask him to leave?

Her troubled gaze shifted left and snagged on the reddening graze high on his cheekbone. Superficial, she decided, but that didn't stop the sudden sick churning in her stomach. What if that fist had really connected? What if his skin had split, or the bone beneath had broken? All because she had waylaid him, had called him back down into that courtyard.

"You need something on that," she said, although the truth was more tangled in her need to treat him than his need of treatment.

"Something?"

"When Joshua progressed from walking to running, he skinned his knee every other day. I have salve. I have plasters."

One corner of his mouth quirked. "They work?"

More relieved by that hint of humor than she had any right to be, Julia smiled. "I'm not sure. I suspect the magic is in the *third* ingredient."

"Which is?"

"I kiss it better."

And because her nerves hadn't entirely settled, because making such a sassy suggestion surprised her almost as much as her aggression had done back in the hotel yard, she turned and walked away.

Relax, she told herself. *You can do this. You like having people in your home. Hospitality is your thing.*

"Come through," she called over her shoulder. "Make yourself comfortable."

He came through, but he didn't bother taking her up on the second part of her offer. Standing dead-center of her minute square of Axminster, legs spread and hands on hips, he made the whole darn room look uncomfortable.

"I'm making tea, if you'd like a cup. Or perhaps you'd prefer a drink, although there's not a lot of choice. We definitely do not run to bourbon." She opened the refrigerator door. "Let's see…there's a half of Chardonnay and some cask Lambrusca, and if you're lucky Kree might have left a beer… Yes, the lucky last!"

Bright smile fixed in place, she held the bottle up for his perusal. He nodded. "I'll try the beer."

That didn't surprise her. He didn't look like a Chardonnay kind of man. Setting the bottle on the table that divided kitchen and living area seemed safer than walking over there and placing it in his hand. That might involve skin contact. Her nerves jumped again. The silence—*his* silence—was getting to her, so she briskly crossed the room and flicked the switch on Kree's stereo.

With each step she felt both his watchfulness and the responsive flare of heat deep in her belly.

"Where *is* Kree?"

"Over at Cliffton, at Tagg's. She's staying over."

Julia hadn't thought it possible, but the implication of Kree staying over at her boyfriend's house wound the tension in the tiny room even tighter. Unbearably so.

The smile she tossed his way fell under the same description. "The things I need are in the bathroom. I won't be long."

In the bathroom, she had to grasp the edge of the basin

while she took several deep breaths. It helped ground her a little. Music started playing in the living room—had she actually selected a CD, or had Zane done that? Interested in what might or might not have been his choice, she listened intently to a lengthy instrumental intro to a bluesy track. Nice. She hoped it *was* his taste.

But when a sultry female voice slunk into the mix, crooning about how she was gonna ''dive on in at the shallow end,'' Julia gave a sardonic little snort. *She* hadn't bothered with the shallow end. Driven by a curious compulsion to do something outside her usual sphere, along with a more familiar longing to fill that yawning hollowness inside, she had dived right in at the deep end. From the very top of the high tower. Without so much as testing the water.

Without a life jacket.

She supposed the new hairdo and a sampling from Kree's cosmetics tray might have provided some sort of buoyancy...or illusion thereof. She turned to the mirror and saw that her make-up was long gone, and as for the sexy new hair—well, it still fell in interesting layers around her face, but it was no more than a new hairstyle.

She thought about how she'd felt with her face snuggled against Zane's chest, with his lips on her throat and his body pressed hard against hers, and she wondered how much of *that* had been an illusion, too. How could he feel so right in her arms, yet so wrong in her living room? It didn't make sense. She supposed she was pretty much floundering. She was definitely out of her depth.

With a heavy sigh, she reached up to open the small cupboard where she stored the first-aid bits and pieces. At least half a dozen boxes and spray packs tumbled out. Shaking her head, she bent to retrieve them. Kree's disposable razors, Kree's deodorant, Kree's Q-Tips, Kree's styling mousse—tidiness was *not* her housemate's strong suit.

After she'd gathered all the escapees and lined them up on the vanity, Julia reached to the back of the middle shelf. And there they were, the tube of salve and a pack of plasters, obviously shoved out of the way by shelf-hogging Kree. She retrieved both and was about to start repacking when she noticed a pack right at the back. A little black box that made her mouth go dry and her pulse skip a beat. She had forgotten all about it....

Zane poured the rest of his beer down the drain. Truth was, he didn't like beer any better than coffee. Truth was, he didn't want to drink anything. That wasn't why he'd followed her inside.

So why did you, bud?

Dumb question, given her come-in-for-coffee crack. His body had jumped to instant attention. Even while his mind was advising him not to get involved, that rigid body was screaming in his other ear. *She wants to jump your bones, and* you're *thinking of going home? Are you nuts?*

Coming to grips with the concept of Julia Goodwin wanting to jump anyone's bones was his problem. He'd tagged her as the virtuous, careful, slow-moving type from the start. Hell, he *knew* she was that type. Maybe the belly button ring qualified as non-standard equipment, but the rest was genuine, top-of-the-line, out-of-his-price-range Good Girl.

What about the way she danced? The way she kissed?

So, okay, he'd been wrong to make assumptions based on how she looked and how she'd been brought up. Wasn't that his exact beef with this town? The fact that it had made up its mind about him twenty years ago and was unprepared to accept that he'd changed? Same as he was doing with her.

Disconcerted by the notion but unsure how far he wanted to pursue it, he searched for somewhere to dispose of his bottle. It took him a while to find the bin, seeing as she'd covered it with a flowery skirt thingamajig. On the outside Julia looked all soft and flowery, like that bin camouflage, but underneath she was one surprise after another.

Tonight she'd shown a quiet strength that was just as seductive to Zane as all that pale-skinned, dawn-scented softness. Back at the Lion, when she'd looked up at him on the stairs, her eyes had smoldered with fury. But she didn't yell. She didn't throw her arms around and stomp her feet. She barely raised her voice.

With a gentle tenacity, she went after what she wanted. The way she sought him out at the bar and then conned him into slow-dancing, the way she followed him and kissed him as though she never wanted to stop—it all pointed to *her* wanting *him.* She hadn't been coy about inviting him inside, either, but once that door clicked shut, *then* she'd pasted on that fake smile and started playing Perfect Hostess.

Make yourself comfortable, she'd said. *What would you like to drink?*

Obviously she'd taken one look at him inside her pretty flower-swathed walls and wondered what she'd been thinking. Right now she was likely sitting on the side of her bathtub biting her lip while she tried to come up with a way to let him down lightly. Because politeness wouldn't allow her to come right out and say it.

I've made a mistake. Turns out I don't want to sleep with you after all.

His whole being bucked at the thought. No, dammit, he wasn't going to give her the chance.

* * *

Her old-fashioned, claw-footed bathtub was exactly as Zane had pictured it…except without Julia perched on its wide rim. She was standing at the sink, stretching on bare feet to replace something in a high cabinet. Her shoes lay discarded to one side.

Clearly she hadn't heard his arrival, and that was okay, because it gave him a chance to study the long exposed line of her sweet-tasting throat, the jut of her breasts outlined by her tightly stretched top and the glimpse of pale midriff bared by her upward stretch.

He must have made some sound—probably a groan, given the sudden painful tightness of his jeans—because she swung around, clearly startled. Flustered, too, because she dropped the box she'd held in her hand, then knocked a couple of other things over in her fumbling attempt at a catch. The box ricocheted off the edge of the basin to land at Zane's feet.

Eyes wide, cheeks flushed the same rosy-pink as her bathroom walls, she started babbling about Kree not packing her things away properly and them all falling out when she opened the door to look for the antiseptic.

Chick stuff, Zane thought. *That's why she's blushing.* It was kinda cute, and he had to battle to keep a straight face. He stooped to retrieve the box, then set it on the edge of the vanity. But he couldn't help noticing it wasn't chick stuff. It was guy stuff.

Condoms, to be precise.

She grabbed the box and shoved it away. Then she bent and picked up the other things she'd knocked over. Put them away in neat soldiery rows, unlike the box she'd juggled into that cupboard as if it were a lump of hot coal. "Kree's stuff," she'd said. Evidence of his kid sister's sex life, which he could do without. Although he should be happy that she was acting smart, that she was practicing safe—

"Why are you so embarrassed if they're Kree's?" he demanded.

"Why do you assume they're hers?" But before he could even think about how to answer, she held up a hand. Her shoulders slumped a little as she let out a long sigh. "Don't bother answering that. It's patently obvious that I'm not used to handling them."

The thought of her hands touching, stretching, rolling…

Zane had to clear his throat of thick, cloying heat before he could speak. "So they *are* Kree's?"

"Actually, they're mine."

If her face grew any hotter, Julia thought, they would have to send the fire brigade to put it out. How had she gotten herself into this discussion? How could she get herself out of it? She raked the hair back from her face and squared her slumped shoulders.

"I bought them a while back and put them away for a rainy day." And that was all she was saying on the matter. "You wanted something? The bathroom, maybe? As you can see, you found it."

"I came to see what was taking so long." He inclined his head toward the first-aid supplies on the vanity. "And to see if you're ready to play nurse."

His jokey tone should have eased Julia's nerves, but he also took two steps into the room and somehow managed to fill all the available space. Perhaps if he were sitting, instead of standing so close…

She pulled out the bathroom stool. "Why don't you take a seat?"

"You want me to sit on that little thing?" He stared at it suspiciously, as if judging whether it would support his weight.

Perhaps he had a point... "Would the edge of the bathtub be better?"

He eyed it with similar mistrust but sat. And stretched out his long legs so Julia had to step around them to fetch the salve.

To apply it, she had to step *between* them.

Oh, dear Lord. Julia took a deep breath. *How do real nurses do this? How do* they *maintain a clinical detachment?*

Perhaps if she thought of him as Joshua—a bigger version, who didn't squirm and chatter nonstop. She turned and almost tripped over one of his feet. At least size fourteen, she thought light-headedly.

No. Thinking of him as a child was definitely too much to ask of her imagination. What she really needed was to keep her imagination occupied. Perhaps some idle chatter of her own would help.

"About my décor," she began, looking around for somewhere to put the lid she'd taken off the salve.

"Here."

He took it, set it on one thigh. *One wide, hard, denim-encased thigh.*

"Your décor?" he prompted.

"You don't like it, do you?"

"Let's just say it's not what I'd choose."

She looked up from squeezing salve onto her finger and caught the teasing light in his eyes. Teasing is good, she thought as her lips curved into an answering smile. So much better than those intense angsty silences.

"It suits you, though," he continued.

"How so?"

"Pretty. Soft. Ladylike."

"I'm not sure how to take that. Tonight I was trying for a completely different look."

"Yeah." His crooked little grin caused her heart to skip a beat. "It sure must be tough being a good girl."

"Tell me about it," she quipped, and when she rolled her eyes for effect, Zane laughed out loud.

Oh, dear Lord, that laughter should be classified as lethal, but then, this man had so many killer qualities. Just standing this close to him was a health threat, and as for the thought of applying the antiseptic....

Wicked wanton images danced across her vision. They all involved her fingers, cool cream and his hot, naked skin.

When she lifted her salve-smeared hand toward his face it was far from steady...until his hand snaked up lightning-fast to circle her wrist.

"I don't need that stuff," he said roughly.

"Oh." Julia became acutely aware of an aura of intense energy emanating from his body. It enfolded her; it steeped her body with restless heat. Yet it also held her in its thrall, like some invisible force field. She moistened her suddenly dry lips. "I don't suppose you want the plaster, either?"

"No." The beat of silence was heavy with expectancy. "But I do need that magic third ingredient."

Need, not want. Heart bounding at a million miles an hour, Julia considered his word choice. He *needed* her kiss, and as she met his straight no-more-teasing look, she imagined that need crying out to her and every lonely unfulfilled place inside her responding.

Oh, yes, Zane, I hear you.

They were inappropriate thoughts, dangerous thoughts, and she tried to dispel them with an ineffectual, "No," which Zane misinterpreted.

"Yes," he insisted, tugging at her wrist until she fell into him—into the widespread vee of his thighs, into the hard wall of his chest, into a kiss that picked up where the first had left off.

His head slanted to the perfect angle, her mouth opened in silent welcome, and any notion of preliminaries flew out the open window. They kissed, Julia decided, with the same unchoreographed harmony as they danced. Now it was tongue sliding against tongue, lips shifting to match lips, teeth nipping and teasing, and all with a slow, soulful synchronicity.

Julia murmured her approval as he moved to her jaw, as he gently bit her earlobe and nuzzled her neck. Then he was kissing her again, kissing her and easing his big hands over her hips, skimming down to catch the hem of her skirt.

To slide underneath.

Work-roughened palms settled on the backs of her naked thighs, and for a long deliberate moment did nothing more. An erotic warmth seeped through Julia's body, an exquisite pleasure that stole her breath. She arched her back, clutched at his shoulders, and when those sure hands commenced a sensual upward slide, desire fisted tight in her belly. She grabbed at his shirt, dragging it from his jeans, and then…oh, yes, *there!* Her hands were on him, on skin stretched taut over corded muscle, on those long, flat planes of his back.

His fingers curled into her buttocks to drag her closer, right into the cradle of his hips, and the kiss changed shape, stretched into a wild and carnal mating of mouths and tongues and shallow breaths. When Julia felt the rigid evidence of his desire, she went a little crazy.

Breaking the kiss, she tore at his shirt with frantic hands, forcing the buttons to give under her relentless attack, making a strangled sound when one caught and held. Mindless, desperate, driven, she took a moment to register his hands on her face, holding her with a calming strength until she stilled.

His eyes were hot and sharply focused. On her. As if she were the core of his concentration, his thinking, his being. She felt a strange ambivalence—a slowing of time and a dulling of external awareness at complete odds with the urgency careering through her blood.

"I want to do this part slowly," he said in that smoke-and-whisky voice. "I want to undress you piece by piece, to see you inch by inch."

She watched his gaze slowly drop, felt it brush over her breasts. Felt them strain tight and uncomfortable against her bra. Clever fingers slid the first button free. When the second popped open at least five seconds later, her breath grew jagged with impatience.

"Couldn't you hurry just a little?"

Zane laughed, and the sound was harsh and strained. Going slow was just about killing him. Button number three eased open, and he sucked in air at the glimpse of pale pink lace. Shoved aside the desperate urge to grab and tear. Despite his rough edges—maybe because of them—he prided himself on handling women with smooth restraint. If they wanted rough treatment, let 'em find it someplace else. That was his motto, had been since the year he left Plenty.

Surprisingly steady fingers moved lower. He would do this with patience and style. By staying civilized. By peeling away her Good Girl clothes in gradual increments to reveal all that soft, supple skin...

All thought evaporated as he opened the last button and peeled back the sides of her blouse. He had imagined how she might look, had dreamed of how she would look, but nothing had prepared him for the reality...or for his response. Not his body's—that was a given—but the clutch of emotion, fierce and strong, in the most elemental of places.

Her skin shimmered in full glossy curves above the lace of her skimpy bra. Skin so finely textured, so translucent, he could see each vein beneath the surface. With the pad of one finger he traced the most distinct blue thread until it disappeared into pink lace, and when he put his mouth there, when he lapped at it with his tongue, she cried out and arched her back.

Need swamped his senses.

He needed to cup those breasts so the pale flesh spilled over the lace, so the nipples pressed hard against his palms. He needed to suckle her, to drag each distended nipple into his mouth, to feed on her little mewling sounds of encouragement. He needed to surge to his feet and push her back against the vanity, to press himself into her softness, to ease the painful pressure in his groin.

It wasn't enough.

Lifting her, spreading her knees so he could move between them, caressing the backs of her calves and the insides of her thighs, none of it was enough. He needed to be where he touched her now, deep inside the wet and wanting place he stroked through her satin panties.

"Zane."

His name slid off her tongue in a soft rush of breath, and he completely lost it. He had to have her before he woke and found it was a dream, before she blinked and realized she'd made a mistake. He caressed her more urgently, felt her desperation in the restless shifting of her hips, in the boneless yielding of her thighs. All he had to do was open his pants, all he had to do—

Abruptly he wrenched himself back, shook his head. *Without protecting her? What was he thinking?*

"Zane?"

She blinked slowly. Gradually her eyes regained focus. He felt her hands on his arms, unconsciously caressing as they slid back and forth over the bulge of his biceps. Her gaze engaged somewhere about shoulder height, and her hands suddenly stilled.

Tension bit down hard as she pulled his shirt—still anchored by that one lone button—aside.

"You have a tattoo."

Her voice wasn't harsh with accusation but soft with discovery, and the tightness in Zane's gut eased a fraction. Her finger traced over the mark, left-right-left, following the simple zigzag shape.

"Lightning never strikes twice in the one place, huh?"

The edge to her smile tugged at Zane's receding tension, cranking it up a notch.

"I told you I wasn't staying in town."

"I heard you." Leaning forward, she pressed her lips to the lightning bolt mark. "Will you stay tonight?"

Her normally clear voice came out a little husky, and when she smiled crookedly, he felt the rasp deep inside. Zane should have heard the warning, the clanging of bells and alarms, but he was too caught up in the beguiling twist to her smile. On anyone else it would have been wicked.

Without taking her eyes from his face, she reached up above her head to open the cabinet door. Zane's gaze flicked to the contents and back to her face. "Rainy day, huh?"

"I think I heard a few drops on the roof."

Zane snorted as he reached over her. "Damn near cats and dogs."

She laughed, a glorious full-bodied sound that rang through his blood as he shoved aside her neatly aligned soldiers to find the hidden box. Her eyes seemed to track it out of the cupboard, though her smile might have tightened a fraction. She definitely swallowed hard. But then she straightened her shoulders and flicked her chin in the direction of the door. "Bedroom?"

"You're sure?"

"Positive."

Six

He didn't bother with the overhead light, and he didn't bother with the bed. Because when he paused in the doorway and caught sight of her window seat, his senses leapt with possibilities and his mind decided with certainty.

There.

He wanted her naked on that bank of plush cushions, framed by the lacy swathe of the curtains and the thick bank of roses outside her bay window. He wanted her lit only by the soft glow from her bedside lamp, which he flicked on. Then he lowered her to the window seat in a long sensual slide, and she hummed her approval.

With unhurried hands he removed her blouse. With unhurried lips he kissed her throat, her shoulders, the rise of her breasts. When he reached around to unhook her bra, he felt her swiftly drawn breath, felt her hands grab at his back, curl into his shirt. And he wanted them on his skin.

"Take my shirt off," he directed.

When they were both naked from the waist up, he pulled her into his arms and kissed her, relishing the pressure of her breasts against his chest. Reveling in the feel of her, the taste of her, the sounds of her escalating passion. He unzipped her skirt and pushed it down her hips so he could skim greedy hands lower, fill them with the roundness of her hips and the swell of her belly.

The breath left his lungs in a violent rush when his fingers snagged in her only piece of jewelry. He'd forgotten…. How could he have forgotten? Gripped by a sudden savage desire to see what his hand had touched, he grabbed her skirt and dragged it over her head. Tossed it behind him. Then he slid from the seat, spreading her knees so he could kneel between them.

At first he sank back on his heels to merely look. With her hair all mussed and her face flushed with arousal, with her eyes clouded by a hazy blend of desire and some other unnamed emotion, she took his breath. His gaze dipped, became distracted by the spectacular sight of her full breasts moving in time with her rapid breathing, before dropping lower…to find what his eyes sought hidden behind her hands.

Behind fingers that twisted as if unsure what to do now that he'd removed himself from her reach.

Hunger and tenderness warred for dominance as he came up onto his knees and put those hands back on him, as they tangled in his hair and pulled him into a deep, deep kiss. While their mouths danced the familiar steps, their hands learned new variations, sliding and skating, dipping and turning, until Zane grew dizzy.

"Enough," he growled into her mouth, but he only meant enough teasing, enough torment. He doubted he could ever have too much of her.

And when he hooked his fingers into her panties and

dragged them down her legs, *she* reached for his zip and tugged it open, freeing his aching sex, stroking it and driving him crazy with the desperation of her hands and her voice.

"Oh, please hurry."

Zane laughed harshly as he searched for and finally located the discarded box. "Believe me, I'm hurrying as fast as I can."

She wrapped her legs around him the instant he was covered, pressing her heat against him, imploring him with the sweetest persuasion. He pushed her back on the cushions and rose above her, hovering at the brink of that first wild plunge to stare fiercely into her eyes, to find the exact moment of connection.

"Now, Zane, oh, please, *now!*"

He thrust deep and strong and felt her surround him, pulling him deeper, welcoming him home. And oh, how he wanted to stay there, so deep inside that he touched her goodness, that he became part of it, that it became part of him. Maybe if he never moved, maybe if he stayed in this exact place…

But she moved impatiently beneath him, reaching up to bite at him with a hungry mouth, pressing her hips to a new angle that screamed at his control. What little control he had left. With a savage curse, he pulled himself back and drove into her again, into her sweetness and her heat. He cupped her breast and flicked his tongue over its distended point, and she widened her knees and lifted her hips, and he touched somewhere deep inside that made her cry out.

"There, oh yes, there," she moaned, and Zane felt sweat bead on his brow as he forced himself to withdraw slowly, to push himself back with restraint. She rolled her hips restlessly, dug her nails into him and demanded more.

Just once more, he told himself through gritted teeth, *and then it's civilised all the way.*

He plunged again, deeper and faster, found that same sweet spot and couldn't stop. Not when she chanted his name over and over, until it echoed in him like a mantra of hope and promise. Not when her climax gripped at him, pulsed around him, until his blood roared in his eardrums and he had to chase after his own release, to find it in one last thundering storm of sensation.

Zane woke with sunlight warm on his face and Julia's soft curves snuggled flush against his side. For a long, sleep-hazy minute he savored the buzz of morning arousal, knowing he had only to dip his head and kiss any one of a dozen sites to spark her husky murmur of approval.

He knew this from experience.

How many times had he turned to her during the night? How many times had she welcomed him into her body and sighed his name in that mind-blowing moment of connection?

Not enough. From one hour to the next, never enough.

That spontaneous answer jangled alarm bells in his head. How could such sublime sex not be enough? He should be lying here boneless, sucked dry, not thinking about starting all over again.

What was it with this woman?

Taking care not to wake her, he smoothed back her tangled mass of hair. And felt a sick, gut-deep jolt as he exposed her face, throat, and breasts…all that pale tender skin marked by his lack of control.

So much for civilized!

He scrubbed a hand over his whisker-rough jaw and swore savagely as he amended his earlier answer. *Too many times. Too many times without restraint.* His feet hit the floor hard. Pausing only to haul on jeans, to grab his shirt and socks and boots, he was halfway to the door before his brain cranked into action.

What the hell was he doing?

He dropped his boots and stared at the scrunched-up shirt in his hands. Noticed prints, chest-high, where Julia had grabbed him with salve-smeared fingers. What he should be doing was rubbing that stuff into her whisker-burned skin—waking her with some consideration, instead of slinking off like…like the unprincipled loser this town had labeled him.

Thoughts of watching her sleepy eyelids flutter open, of witnessing that first unguarded moment of wakefulness, took a firm grip on his imagination. Yeah, that was what he wanted. To surprise her—maybe with the cup of tea he'd deprived her of last night.

Kissing that surprise from her lips would be a pleasurable side benefit.

Decision made, he shoved arms into shirtsleeves, feet into boots, and headed for the kitchen. Making morning-after breakfast would be a ground-breaking experience, but then, so was Julia. Everything about Julia. That disquieting concept sobered his spirits as he peered into the refrigerator. Later he would examine what it meant. Right now he needed to concentrate on breakfast…or he would after a run to the corner store for supplies.

Zane shook his head disgustedly as he closed the fridge door. No eggs, no bacon, no bread. And the only milk was that weak-as-water stuff women seemed to think was good for them. Not that Julia had come to any harm, he decided as he let himself out the front door. *Her* curves were still in perfect order. Lush, full, inviting. Curves designed to lure a man to the edge of sanity, then drive him over the edge.

The sound of a car decelerating called his attention, reluctantly, to the street. The car—four-cylinder, missing on one—pulled up opposite the front gate. A door slammed, and seconds later his sister swung into view. Three rapid strides later she saw him on the veranda and delight chased the distracted frown from her face.

"Zane! What are you doing here?"

Sharp blue eyes took in his unbuttoned shirt and bed-mussed hair, then flicked in the direction of Julia's bedroom. Her overnight bag hit the path with a thud before she advanced on him with strides that gathered length and speed and fury with each successive footfall. By the time she'd taken the three steps as one, pulled back her arm and landed one on his arm, the punch carried ten times the power of last night's drunken assailant.

"What in heaven's name do you think you're doing?" she snarled.

Unsure how to answer—was she mad about him being here, or mad because he appeared to be leaving?—Zane chose the safe option. Silence. And played for sympathy. He flexed his fingers and extended his elbow, stretching the cramped muscle that had taken the blow.

Her eyes followed the gesture, but her narrowed gaze lacked contrition. It skimmed over his face and came to rest on his cheekbone. "I hope Julia did that."

He lifted a hand and fingered the tender spot. "Because...?"

"You have to ask?"

Yes, he had to ask. He had no idea what bug had crawled up Kree's butt, although it was obviously a big, surly brute. With teeth. "Not that it's any of your business, but when Julia invited me to stay, it wasn't for sparring practice."

"*Julia* invited *you* to stay? And you didn't see anything wrong with that picture?"

Zane ignored a strong twinge of unease. "Not from where I was standing."

"Then let me clear your vision. Julia doesn't bring men home. She doesn't do one-night stands. She's looking for a husband, for heaven's sake, not a good time in the sack!"

"Then the Lion's a damn fool place to be looking."

"She went to the Lion? Oh, man." Kree closed her eyes for a moment before muttering, "She actually took me up on that frog-hunting business."

"Frog-hunting?"

"It's a private joke."

All kinds of misgivings knotted Zane's gut, and he knew they wouldn't leave him alone until he found out what was going on here. Dipping down to Kree's height, he took hold of her upper arms and looked right into her eyes. "Why did she go to the Lion?"

"Temporary insanity?"

Zane tightened his grip.

"I was only half joking." She blew out a ragged sigh. "I guess she was feeling…I don't know…like she needed validation as a woman."

"That makes about as much sense as the frog business. What's going on, Kree?"

"Shouldn't you be asking Julia?"

"I'm asking you."

"Look, she just found out that her ex is having a baby, so she's feeling a bit vulnerable, okay?"

Her ex. The man she'd been married to. Despite a growing chorus of *don't-go-there*'s, he had to ask. "She still loves him?"

"Hardly."

Intense relief silenced his misgivings and encouraged

him to pursue the next thought. If she didn't love this guy... "Why is the baby such an issue?"

"I'm going to regret this." Kree rolled her eyes. "Who am I kidding? I regret this already, but you're not going to let up on me, are you?"

"No."

"That's what I thought." She took an audible breath, and Zane eased his grip, then ran his hands down her arms soothingly, encouraging her to continue. "She did love Paul at one time. She loved him enough to want a baby with him—to want it more than anything—but he sweet-talked her into waiting, even though it damn near broke her heart. And now, before the ink's dry on the marriage licence, he's got his new wife pregnant. How do you imagine that made Julia feel?"

Zane didn't want to even start imagining how Julia felt. Safer to concentrate on how *he* felt. Which was like the dumbest kind of sap for thinking she wanted *him*, when anyone with a healthy dose of testosterone would have done. He'd actually thought she'd want him hanging around in the morning, bringing her breakfast in bed, for Pete's sake!

Hadn't he learned anything from Claire Heaslip?

Keeping the cold edge of bitterness from his voice proved pretty much impossible. "She should be feeling lucky she didn't have that baby, or right now she'd be coping with junior on her own."

"Don't go comparing Julia with our mother," Kree said gently. "She's custom made for the role. Her child wouldn't grow up like we did."

That went without saying, but every kid deserved a crack at two parents—given that they weren't total screw-ups like his and Kree's. "Yeah, well, there isn't any child, so how about we drop it?"

His sister's eyes narrowed suddenly. "You *were* careful, right?"

Zane rocked back on his heels. He couldn't believe what she was asking, couldn't believe she had the hide to question him on birth control. Couldn't believe that he was reliving—vividly—that one unguarded minute in the pre-dawn hours... Less than a minute before he came fully awake, before sanity prevailed.

He felt heat in his cheekbones, heard it in his voice. "That's none of your business."

"You're right. I'm sorry, Zane."

"Yeah, you and me both."

He regretted the words as soon as they left his mouth, but it was too late to take them back. Understanding already softened Kree's expression. "Oh, Zane. What have you gone and done?"

What *had* he gone and done? Self-disgust made him answer more harshly than he intended. "I got myself laid, okay? Something I haven't done often enough lately."

Kree's eyes widened in shock. Tough. She had started this, so she could hear him out.

"What did you expect to hear? That we fell—"

"That's enough, Zane."

Kree spoke right over the top of him; her eyes looked right past him. An uneasy sensation tickled the back of his neck. Hell.

Julia was already backing away. She wanted to keep on retreating all the way to her bedroom, where she could quietly lie down and die. But he turned, their eyes met, and pride held her firm, made her lift her chin and forced some kind of smile to her lips.

"Sorry if I interrupted," she said as she pushed the screen door open and came out onto the veranda. Focusing on Kree made it marginally easier to fake a breezy attitude.

"I heard voices when I woke and wondered who was here. I thought you were going straight from Tagg's to work."

"Yeah, well, we had a disagreement, and I decided he could get his own breakfast." Kree shrugged casually. Her relationships always traveled rocky ground. She always bounced back. "Speaking of which, I'm starved. Anyone care to join me for breakfast?"

Her concerned gaze met Julia's and asked the question she hadn't voiced. *Are you okay?* Julia hoped her smile looked more natural than it felt. "I'd love a cup of tea."

"Zane?"

"Another time. I've got work to do."

"At seven on a Saturday?"

"That's right."

Julia chanced a glance in his direction and connected with a flat, cold expression she felt to her marrow. Rubbing her hands up and down her arms didn't help. She turned on her heel and would have walked back inside if he hadn't stopped her with a lightning-fast hand on her arm.

Lightning-fast. With unerring precision, her gaze slid to the tattoo exposed by his unbuttoned shirt, and she recalled the frisson of foreboding she'd felt the first time she'd seen it. She should have heeded that warning. *Zap, and he's gone.*

"Can I have a word?"

"Would that word be goodbye?" she asked with a cynical half smile.

Something stirred in the tricky depths of his eyes before they flicked past her, presumably to Kree. "Beat it, short stuff."

Kree muttered something unintelligible, at least to Julia. She was too busy marshalling her defenses. She closed her eyes, heard the door smack shut behind Kree, felt nothing but the fraught atmosphere that closed around her, dragging the air from her lungs. And when she took a necessary breath, it was filled with memories.

Because he stood too close, shirt unbuttoned, skin bare. *Oh, this was too unfair!*

On the brink of hearing his so-long-it's-been-fun monologue, all she could think about was leaning into his chest. Wrapping her arms around his waist. She wrapped them around herself instead.

"Are you cold?"

"No." Then, hating her own dishonesty, she amended the answer. "Perhaps a little."

"You want to move into the sun?"

"Why not?"

At the far end of the veranda, where the early morning sun burst through the foliage in fragmented pools of light, she lifted her face. Felt the gentle warmth touch her eyelids and waited for it to seep into her flesh. It didn't. All she felt was the confusing intensity of his gaze, the weight of the lengthening silence, and she couldn't stand it any longer. "What is it you wanted to say?"

"Why did you go to the Lion last night?"

She pushed her hands into the pockets of her robe. Feigned a careless shrug. "I felt like going out."

"Cut the crap, Julia. You've never been in that bar in your life."

He employed the same blunt tone she'd overheard from the hallway, and it reminded her of his words. As if they'd ever stopped whirring through her brain. *I got myself laid, okay? Something I haven't done often enough lately.*

A humorless smile twisted her lips. "Perhaps I was looking for the same thing as you were."

"Kree said you're looking for a husband. That's hardly the same thing. Marriage isn't top of my priority list."

Julia felt herself flush. "I'm not asking you to marry me. That's not what I wanted from you."

"What *did* you want? That baby you're so keen on?"

Julia pressed a hand to her temple. "I can't believe she told you that."

"Don't blame Kree. I pressured her, so she told me you were bent out of shape about your ex's baby."

Comprehension finally dawned. "And you think I deliberately set out to pick you up, that I slept with you because I wanted to get pregnant?"

"Yes, I do think you deliberately set out to pick me up. What I'm trying to establish is why."

"Obviously because I'm so bent out of shape!"

He blew out an exasperated breath before turning away to stare into the middle distance. And, God help her, she felt herself drifting closer, lifting a hand toward the stiff column of his back, forming the words to tell him…to tell him what? That she'd slept with him because she couldn't resist? That she'd experienced something unprecedented, something huge and wonderful? That she'd woken this morning thinking her world had changed?

He turned abruptly, fixed her with a hard, silvery glare, and her hand fell ineffectually back to her side.

"Why me, Julia? Do I look like the kind of man who likes being used? Do girls like you get a kick out of suckering us lower life forms?"

Beyond the sharp bite of his voice, deeper than the angry colour that traced his high cheekbones all the way to the corners of his eyes, she felt his hurt. Knew she had to reach out to him, to explain how it had really been.

"I didn't use you, Zane," she said evenly. "I went to the Lion because I wanted you."

"Because you wanted sex with me."

She lifted one shoulder in an uncomfortable half shrug. How could she explain that it was more than that?

He didn't give her a chance. He fired one last bitter salvo—"Then I guess we both got what we wanted"— before he turned and strode away.

She didn't intend to leave it at that, but he needed time to cool down, and she needed time to assemble her tumultuous thoughts. Her morning shift at Gracey's seemed endless, and Bill's shop was closed when Julia got there. The teenage pump attendant hadn't seen Zane. "But I only started at eleven. Bill's out back having lunch. He might've seen him."

Julia picked her way up the path beside the garage and knocked on the door of the residence. Waited a few seconds, then knocked more loudly.

"Hold your horses. I hear you. No need to put—" Bill stopped complaining when he swung the door open and saw her on the stoop. "Julia."

"I'm sorry to disturb you. Grant said I'd find you here."

Bill waved her apology aside. "You got car trouble?"

"No. Actually, I wanted to talk to you about something else. If you don't mind?"

"I don't mind someone to talk to besides myself. Come on in." He stepped aside and waved her past. "You want coffee? A cold drink?"

"No, I'm fine, thank you." Julia followed him into a tiny living room crammed with mismatched furniture.

"Have a seat."

Bill scooped an armful of newspapers and magazines from an ancient two-seater, and Julia sat. She shifted away from a protruding spring before sinking lopsidedly into the sofa's depths.

"So, what did you want to talk about?" Bill lowered his lanky frame into an armchair.

"I'm looking for Zane, actually. I don't suppose you know where I'd find him?"

Bill checked the wall clock. "At the rate he drives, you'd find him 'round about two hundred thirty miles down the road."

"He's gone?"

"That he is. Called in on his way out of town, just so I'd know."

"That was sudden."

Bill humphed his agreement. "That's Zane. Sudden."

Oh, yes, Julia silently agreed. Suddenly there, turning her world upside down. Suddenly gone, without setting it right. Not that he hadn't warned her. Twice he'd told her he was leaving. She simply hadn't allowed the reality to sink in.

"My own fault, I suppose, for teaching him everything I know. Turned him into a damn fine grease monkey— almost as good as me," Bill ruminated. "Stands to reason there's always someone wanting to give him a job."

"Is that why he left? For work?"

"Some mate had him lined up to fill in when he took leave. That's how he came to have a week to fill here."

"Oh." And with that one soft sound Julia's hopes dissolved. He hadn't left suddenly because of an emergency, he'd left according to plans made before he arrived in town. He must have known that he was leaving today, yet he hadn't bothered to say goodbye.

"Can't say I won't miss his help around here."

"Perhaps *you* should offer him a job," she suggested dryly.

"Don't you think I haven't tried? Boy won't even consider it. Town's got too many bad memories."

"Because of the trouble he got into?"

"Which particular trouble?" Bill shook his head. "If you mean the vandalism thing, he got over that real quick when he started working here. Paid off the damage and never looked back. But as for that business with...what was her name? Heaslip girl, family built that pink pile of bricks up on the hill..."

"Claire."

Bill scratched his chest as he considered the name. "Claire, you reckon? A real piece of work, that one."

According to rumor, she had played Zane against a law student from one of the town's upwardly mobile families, and Zane had lost. In a notorious altercation outside that pink pile of bricks, he'd allegedly punched out the college boy and Claire's councilor father, although the story had likely been embellished in the retelling.

Aware that Bill was watching her oddly, that questions were starting to form on his mobile face, she boosted herself out of the butt-consuming sofa. "I'd best be going. Thanks for your time."

"Wish I could have been more help," Bill said as he escorted her to the door.

"Well, you could hardly produce him out of your hip pocket." She lifted a hand in farewell and hurried off down the path.

Her pace didn't slow until she had fetched Mac from the yard and covered the three miles to the riverside reserve in record time. Then she forced herself to sit, to take a few deep breaths, to evaluate the intense disappointment churning through her.

It was irrational to feel let down. She had invited him into her home and into her bed knowing he was leaving; she shouldn't have expected anything more. Now he was gone from town, gone from her life, and there was no place for disappointment. Or regret. He had been an amazing interlude, an unforgettable experience, and she should be feeling…grateful.

Yes, grateful.

Because when he focused all that hard-edged sexuality on her, when he looked at her as if she were the sun at the center of his universe, when he loved her with such single-minded purpose, he had made her feel things she'd never felt before. Such as pure unadulterated feminine power.

She lifted her head and refused to go any further down the list of things he'd made her feel. Strong was enough, especially when she'd been weak for so long.

All her life trying to please others. Her parents, Paul, Chantal. Bending to their wills, their wants, because it was easier than standing up for herself. Well, last night she had gone after what *she* wanted, and if she could do it once, then why not again? Only next time she would choose something less ephemeral than a one-night stand, something with more purpose and more future.

After her divorce she'd dreamed of starting her own business—a cottage industry of some kind, or a nursery. Perhaps even a garden design or landscaping business. But it had remained a dream because she'd never had the strength of character to do anything about it.

Why not now? Why not at least attempt to turn the dream into reality?

It would take some planning, some time, and, yes, a little strength of character, but it might also prove more achievable than her only other post-divorce goal. Because after last night, after Zane O'Sullivan, she had a very strong feeling that all Chantal's potential husbands would seem even more like frogs.

Seven

Julia kicked off her shoes and slumped against the front door she had just closed at her back. Despite its solid support, it took an effort to hold herself upright, to stop herself sliding into a heap on the floor. Once down there, she might never find the strength to haul herself back up again—that was how weighty and enervated she felt. The first she could blame on Chantal's Easter Sunday feast, the second had become her regular condition, but she was learning to live with it.

For the past seven weeks she had felt tired all the time. Too tired to do much about those dreams she'd gotten all fired up about the day Zane left town. Oh, she had tried, but between fitful sleeping and a punishing work schedule, she had managed to exhaust her body, her mind and her enthusiasm.

The work schedule she could justify. Extra shifts, especially at weekends, meant a fatter paycheque. Already the savings account for her prospective business had doubled. And she didn't mind working long hours, more days. Since Kree had suddenly decided to leave her business in the capable hands of her assistant so she could trek through Southeast Asia, the house seemed too quiet, too empty.

Plus work, and/or weariness from work, provided the perfect excuse whenever Chantal rang to arrange a date with her latest Marry Julia prospect. She hadn't yet found the energy to tell Chantal to back off. Drifting with the tide seemed so much easier than swimming against it.

On one disastrous occasion her sister had caught her at a particularly weak moment. A lonely moment. She shouldn't have agreed to the date with Tim; she shouldn't have fallen asleep on the drive home; and she definitely shouldn't have let him kiss her. In that first disoriented moment of wakening, her lips had felt bereft. *She* had felt bereft. Except it wasn't any man's lips she craved. She had been spoiled, inexorably, by one February night.

Her whole life might have been inescapably changed by one miraculous moment during that hot summer night.

She pressed a hand to her belly and failed to suppress the spontaneous surge of elation. Premature, she warned herself. Don't go presuming. Stress had always played havoc with her cycle. Plus there'd been no nausea, no dizziness, nothing but the constant tiredness and an intuitive whisper of certainty.

Or was it merely optimism?

Tomorrow she would drive over to Cliffton and buy a test kit. Tomorrow night she would know. Until then, she refused to allow herself to consider the implications.

Mustering strength, she pushed herself away from the door and headed for the kitchen, out of habit more than anything. As she crossed the living room, the same kind of habit called her gaze to the answering machine. Its blinking eye of light caused her heart to miss a beat, then attempt to catch up with a rush of anticipatory hope.

Every day—every single one of the last forty-nine days—her heart had responded that way, only to be disappointed when the caller turned out to be Chantal or Mitch or her parents calling from Europe. With a disgusted, "Whoever you are, you can just hang on to your britches," she boiled the kettle and made chamomile tea, then carried it through to a comfortable chair.

But that infernal light wouldn't let her relax. *Look at me,* it blinked. *Answer me.* Blink. *Talk to me.* Blink. She struck the play button with unholy force. "There! Are you happy now?"

At the first husky word her whole body jolted. Burning hot tea slopped over the rim of her cup, and, cursing her involuntary reaction, she dashed to the kitchen and stuck her hand under the cold water tap.

Yet somehow she managed to hear every word.

"Kree, what's the point having a cell phone when it's never switched on? Call me. It's urgent."

She replayed the message—twice—but only to ensure that she correctly transcribed his number. Then she replayed it again, this time to catch the various shades of his voice. He sounded strained, not with the frustration of being unable to find Kree, but with something else.

A phantom hint of worry, anxiety, or...pain?

She stared at the carefully printed numbers on the slip of paper in her hand, and her pulse skittered erratically. How urgent was urgent? Did he even know that Kree was out of the country? It wouldn't surprise her if he didn't— they often went months without contact. She didn't understand how they coped with such sporadic communication, with not knowing if the other was hurt or in trouble.

Call me. It's urgent.

Julia glanced at the kitchen clock, moistened her lips and reached for the phone.

"I go get Mummy."

Julia checked the number again, although she knew she'd dialled it correctly, digit by painfully uncoordinated digit. So why had a child answered? A very young child, who now seemed to be squabbling over possession of the receiver with someone called *Krish-eeee.*

Then, thank you God, a distinctly adult voice asked, "Who is it, Jay?"

"Shum lady."

She had seven seconds—she counted them—for the implications to turn leaden in her stomach. A woman. With young children. At the number Zane had left in his message. *Don't jump to conclu—*

"Hello? Are you still there?"

Julia clutched the receiver more tightly in her damp palm. "Yes, hello. I'm looking for Zane O'Sullivan."

"Zane? Oh, he's not here right now but— *Put that down right now, Krissie!* I can take a message."

"Oh. Yes. I'm returning his call to his sister."

Julia paused while the woman repeated her warning to Krissie, this time more forcefully. "Sorry about that. You have kids?"

"Not yet."

"My advice is keep it that way." Her dry chuckle was edged with exasperation. "Zane's sister...that'd be Kree, right?"

"Yes. Zane left a message on the answering machine."

"Did he tell you about his accident?" The woman must have heard Julia's sharp intake of breath, because her tone softened dramatically. "Now, hon, it's nothing to get in a tizz about. You know that knee he banged up back in high school? Well, he managed to do a real job on it this time.''

"How...?" That was all Julia could get out. She felt as weak and quavery as that one word sounded.

"He was rescuing Jay from this big old tree we have out back. I swear, the boy's half mountain goat, climbing anything that stands still long enough. Anyway, Zane went up the tree after him, and the branch gave way. He landed awkwardly, and it just kinda snapped.''

"It's...broken?"

"Not bones—some ligament or other. But the op went real good, so take a deep breath and relax. He's fine. Truly.''

"His message—" Julia took the deep breath, but she couldn't relax. "He said it was urgent.''

"He has this thing about making more work for me. Now he can't do Gav's job at the garage, being on crutches and all, he thinks he should leave. God knows, he's more than enough help keeping these demons out of my hair while I'm nursing the baby. Not that he *needs* to do anything to be welcome here. He's Gav's best mate, and we all love him to death, but you know what he's like when he sets his mind on something. *Jay, please get down from there. Now!*"

Julia lifted a hand to her temple. The woman talked like a dervish—keeping up was making her head spin. Three children now, including a baby. And Gav would be...her husband? A friend of Zane's with a garage—perhaps the one he'd arranged to sub for while he took leave. Paternity leave? It made sense.

"Sorry about that. Now, where were we?"

Through the receiver, Julia heard the faint but distinct squall of a baby. The woman shushed it, and that purely maternal sound of comfort played all over Julia's rocky emotions. Tears pricked at the back of her throat, and she quickly rose to her feet. She shook her head to clear the persistent imagery—Zane rescuing a small boy, Zane cradling a tiny babe—and moistened her dry mouth.

"He can stay with me while his knee mends. I'll come and get him."

"You do what you have to, hon, but he's welcome to stay here as long as he likes. *No, Jay!*"

"You have your hands full—I think it's best. If I can just get some directions…?"

"We're easy to find. You got a pen?"

Finding them had been easy. Prising her foot from the brake pedal so she could negotiate the last hundred meters of driveway…*that* was the difficult part.

Julia blew out a ragged breath. After four hours at the wheel she needed to get out, to stretch, to ease all the kinks of tension from her back and her neck and her limbs. Of course, most of her tension came not from the driving but from anxiety.

After hanging up the phone the previous evening, she realized she hadn't exchanged names with Zane's friend's wife. And the more times she replayed the conversation in her mind, the more obvious it became—she'd almost certainly been mistaken for Kree.

In that neat brick house up on the rise, Zane would be waiting for his sister. How would he react when Julia drove up? She didn't know what to expect, or how she would deal with the awkwardness.

"Awkwardness, schmawkwardness," she muttered. She'd been over the situation a zillion times. Her best friend's brother needed rescuing, and she was the only available white knight. Kree would do the same for her if it were Mitch needing help.

Their one-night history was irrelevant. As was the for-
tuitous timing.

Ignoring the erratic thumping of her heart, she squared
her shoulders and gave herself a pep talk. "Okay, Julia.
You can't sit here for the rest of the century. Get to it."

From the front porch of Gav and Lisa's neat brick house,
Zane watched the stationary vehicle with growing testi-
ness. Had she stalled it? Flooded the engine with her usual
impatience? He didn't recognize the car—it wasn't her
baby Mazda but a large sedan, which might explain the
fact that it wasn't moving. On a compatibility scale of one
to ten, Kree and cars rated a low one. And that was with
cars she knew.

Still, she had thought to borrow something that looked
more reliable and more comfortable than her match-box
toy. He should be thankful for that. If she ever got her butt
into gear and made it up the hill, he would thank the hell
out of her. He hopped to the edge of the porch and was
studying Gav's home-made steps when the screen door
behind him creaked open.

"Don't even think about it," a cheerful voice advised.

"These steps are a disgrace. Why didn't you make a
handrail?"

"Because I envisioned the day, my friend, when you'd
be tempted to do something rash. And detrimental to the
mending of that knee." Gav pulled over a chair. "Here,
take a load off."

"I'll be sitting for the rest of the day."

"Point." Gav followed the direction of Zane's narrow-
eyed gaze. "That your sister?"

"You expecting anyone else?"

"Nah."

Finally the sedan started to move, and Zane tracked its steady approach with a weird sense of foreboding.

''Don't know a soul who drives a Benz,'' Gav drawled finally. ''How about you?''

''It's hurting, isn't it?''

Eyes closed, teeth gritted, Zane didn't bother answering.

''Would it be better if I drove more slowly? Or I could stop and let you rest a while.''

When she eased off the accelerator, he responded immediately. Emphatically. ''No. Don't stop. Keep driving.''

Quicker would be nice. Anything to get me out of this.

Three hours. Three more bloody hours of solicitous questions and sidelong glances. Feigning sleep hadn't helped. Every time she turned those pitying eyes his way, he felt it in every cell of his body. Felt it until he damn near wanted to open the door and jump out. Forget what *that* would do to his knee.

The trip had shaped up as torture from the start, when she'd slid those long legs out of her parents' Merc and their glazes clashed for one intense moment. There were no words of greeting, no smiles of welcome, nothing but a complex blend of sensation and emotion arcing between them. She'd turned away quickly, but he couldn't stem the scalding tide of memories. When she'd smiled at Gav, he'd seen the wicked curve of another smile, felt its hot pressure on his neck. When she'd laughed at Lisa's dry greeting, he'd seen the white flash of her teeth, felt their sweet nip on his shoulder.

Would his traitorous body never let him forget?

He'd stomached the introductions, explanations and invitations—''Have lunch with us, you can't turn around and head straight back''—in silence, while his brain had searched for alternatives. Come up empty. She'd provided the only available means of getting out of Gav and Lisa's hair.

But the last thing he needed was to feel beholden to Julia Goodwin. He would accept her lift back to Plenty, to Bill's place, and that was it. He'd accepted it, but he didn't have to like it. In fact, with every passing mile he found more reasons to *dis*like it.

Take her motive for coming to fetch him. "Kree's my best friend. It's the least I can do," she'd told Lisa with a smile bordering on martyrdom. Yep, Zane just loved being treated like a mission of mercy. He hated it almost as much as being incapacitated, but not half as much as being treated as an object of pity.

That one took him back to his first months in Plenty, when every do-gooder worth their salt wanted to dispense charity to "those poor O'Sullivan children." And here he was, twenty years later, returning to that same damn place, needing to accept the same kind of help, because there was no other option.

Why did it have to be *her?*

Stifling a groan, he rubbed a hand over his jaw, felt the concerned touch of her gaze. Again.

"Would you like to take a painkiller? I have some water in the—"

"No."

"Lisa said you—"

"Which part of *no* didn't you get?"

Zane turned and glared. It was the first time he'd really looked at her since enduring the humiliation of her helping him into the car. Like an invalid. And through the dull-edged pain, beyond his sharper-edged irritation, he noticed she seemed drawn. Skin even paler than he remembered. Smudges under her eyes. Hurt clouding those eyes as she quickly refocused them on the road.

Hell.

"I didn't mean to snap at you," he relented.

"It's okay. You must be feeling every bump in the road."

"Not with this suspension."

She looked pleased. "Then I'm glad I brought the beast. I hate driving it, but I thought it'd be more comfortable, with the bigger seats and the extra leg room."

Her gaze slid down, searing his legs and the general area of his seat with instant heat. He shut his eyes and gritted his teeth. Tried to concentrate on the pain, on despising her pity, on the possible reasons for her tiredness. On anything but the way his body responded to her presence.

In that regard, nothing had changed in the past seven weeks. Not one damned thing.

They drove into Plenty two hours and fifty-six minutes later. "You can drop me at Bill's," he said shortly.

"I told you back at your friends' place—Kree's room is empty, and she would want you to have it."

"Back there I didn't want to argue. I'm staying with Bill."

"You're going to sleep on his too short sofa? With that knee?" Her gaze swung his way for a long second. It held no compassion this time, just a quiet strength. "Or do you intend kicking Bill out of his bed?"

"I'll buy a bed."

"And put it where? You and I both know Bill doesn't have room to swing a wrench."

Zane set his jaw. "Then I'll get a room at the Lion."

"With all those steps?"

"*You* have steps."

"Not at the back door," she countered mildly.

"Then I'll try the new motel."

"You're welcome to try, but I know everywhere's booked up for the Hobbs reunion."

She eased the big car along the curb and cut the engine. The late-afternoon street was empty, the roomy interior of the car silent...except for the noise of frustration grinding away in his brain. If he couldn't handle sharing a car for a few hours, how could he share her house? A bathroom where he'd spread her thighs, where he'd first touched the damp heat—

"I can understand what you're thinking—"

"I doubt it."

"—but it needn't be awkward," she continued, as if she hadn't heard his interjection. Her calm, even tone was starting to irritate him more than if she'd screeched and wailed. "I've already made up your room and bought extra food. I start work at eight in the morning, and I'm currently rostered for a lot of shifts, so I won't be around much."

"Why?"

She blinked slowly. "I thought I just explained. I'm working late almost every day."

"I mean, why are you working so many shifts?"

"Why does anyone work?" she asked with a little shrug.

"Did Kree leave you in the lurch?"

"Oh, no, she paid months in advance—that's not why I need the money. I'm saving for something."

He remembered the day in her yard, when she'd told him she was saving to build a fence. A fence to keep her brother's dog in. And he remembered her terse response when he'd tried to point out *that* inequity. It wasn't something that needed debating now, not with her looking ready to drop with exhaustion and his knee aching like a bitch. She needed to get out of the car. He needed to get his leg elevated.

He released a small measure of banked frustration in a long, ragged sigh. Not resignation, he told himself, but inevitability. "I'll take Kree's room, but only if we come to terms."

"What kind of terms?"

"I'll look after myself. I'll pay board. And I'll build that damn fence for you."

A puzzled look narrowed her gaze. "Fence?"

"The Mac-proof fence."

She shook her head. Puffed out a disbelieving laugh. "Oh, no, absolutely not."

Zane stared back at her, unrelenting. "Take it or leave it."

"And if I leave it?"

"I'll pick up my crutches and hop down to Bill's."

One corner of her mouth lifted in a hint of a smile. "And what if Bill won't have you?"

"He will. He'll give me his bed and move down to the Lion himself."

As he watched her digest that possibility, he felt the power shift like a double shuffle. He knew he'd won. The sharp thrust of satisfaction felt very good.

"Okay," she said slowly. "You can look after yourself, and you can pay some rent. But you are definitely not to go near that fence. You can't possibly do it with your knee."

"No?" Zane smiled with grim determination as he released his seat belt. "Just watch me."

Eight

Julia let him believe she'd caved because it got him out of the car and into her house. Pain had etched tense grooves beside his mouth and tinged his skin with pallor, but she knew he was stubborn enough to grab those crutches and hop all the way down to Bill's. Or as far as he made it before he collapsed.

She understood why he'd felt compelled to make the "deal," that pride wouldn't allow him to accept her help without some sort of contribution, but that didn't make her any more comfortable with accepting his three provisos. Point One: how could he look after himself in his present condition? Point Two: Kree had already paid for the room. Point Three: it was her yard, her fence, her responsibility.

For the next four days she quietly fretted over how she could squirm out of the agreement, which at least gave her something to occupy her mind…something other than the pregnancy issue. She had decided to leave the test until the weekend, when she had time for both the trip to Cliff-ton *and* to deal with the results. When Zane had had time to settle in and become a tad more comfortable in her home and with her company. By the weekend they might actually be conversing.

It was his knee, she reasoned, making him so irritable. And it was only compassion, a natural empathy for any person or creature in pain, that caused the burning ache in her heart every time she saw him wince or pale. Yet he still insisted on doing for himself. No matter how tactfully she offered, her assistance was always curtly refused.

Every evening she approached her house with trepidation, worried over what she mind find in her yard. Zane slumped over a shovel. Zane buried under a collapsed pile of fence panels. Zane carted off to hospital because he'd done some irreparable damage to his knee.

Instead she would find him in the kitchen chopping vegetables, or watching television while something simmered on the stove. And when she found him there, every day looking in a little less pain and a lot less likely to take a finger off, her whole self gladdened.

That troubled her.

On Friday evening, after they'd eaten and cleared up to the accompaniment of their usual stilted conversation, he asked what kind of fence she had in mind. She noted how he was putting weight on his injured leg, and she noted the stubborn set to his jaw when she prevaricated. It was time to do something herself before he made good on his promise.

When Mitch phoned later that night, it was like some kind of wake-up call. He asked after Mac, and she did what she should have done in the first place.

"He's fine, but I do have a favor to ask."

"Hello, my self-sufficient sister needs assistance? I take it there's a blue moon tonight?"

She pictured the wry twist of her brother's grin and felt her own smile spread from deep inside. Mitch had the gift of making her feel good. "I have a problem with Mac getting out of the yard. I want to build a new fence, but I've tied my savings up in a fixed deposit, so—"

"How much? Would two cover it?"

Julia grimaced. "I was hoping for a little more."

"What are you building, a fence or a prison wall? I'll send three thousand, okay?"

"Three *thousand?* Oh, dear Lord. I thought you meant *hundred.* I'll get a quote. It won't be anything like that much."

"Just get it built and send me the bill."

"It's only a loan."

"Whatever."

She pictured his dismissive shrug and smiled. "I might just make it a prison wall, seeing as you're so intent on throwing money my way."

"I'm not throwing cash around. That's Annabel's speciality."

Had she imagined the sharp edge to his voice? "How is your better half?" she asked carefully.

"Last time I saw her, she seemed fine. You wanna hear what Joshua did yesterday?"

Julia lapped up the latest news of her nephew; then the conversation drifted around to their parents' travels, before ending with a lengthy debate on the Crocs' chances for their first NBL pennant. It was only after she'd settled back in bed that she recalled the edge to Mitch's voice when he spoke of Annabel. Were they having marriage troubles? She chided herself for jumping at shadows. Their careers kept them apart for long periods. That was all.

* * *

The next day she finished work at two and immediately called at the hardware store next door to Gracey's to pick up brochures on fencing materials. Walking home with the sun warm on her back and an autumn breeze plucking at the loose flare of her skirt, she felt better than she had in a long time. Still tired, but with a heavy-limbed lassitude instead of her usual bone-weary exhaustion.

She strolled into her yard in that dozy state, but when she rounded the corner of the house and came across Zane, her senses switched to full alert. He was sitting on one of her garden benches, his injured leg propped on the second bench. Head tipped back, eyes closed, he hadn't seen her. A stimulating hum of excitement stirred her blood as she approached with slow, lawn-muted steps.

For the first time all week, she had licence to look her fill.

He wore a sleeveless T-shirt. Or, more accurately, a T-shirt with the sleeves ripped out. One of his arms hung loosely at his side, his fingertips skimming the top of Mac's head. She hadn't even noticed the dog, asleep at his feet.

Was it any wonder?

Her gaze tracked his other arm, lingering on the sun-gilded hair that dusted his sinewy forearm, on the long-fingered hand wrapped around a soft drink can. The can itself rested on his flat belly. She took another three steps closer. Noticed the movement of his thumb, tracing lazy circles in the condensation on the side of the can.

Oh, Lord.

The intense flash of heat cleared everything from her brain. Everything except the memory of that thumb tracing a similar pattern on the curve of her sweat-damp breast.

She pressed a cooling hand to her forehead for a long moment before reality bit.

That measured movement meant he wasn't asleep.

Her guilty gaze jumped to his face, to the shadowy hint of silver-grey watching her through slitted lids. Her hand slipped from forehead to nose to cover her mouth. She must have made some sound, because Mac woke with a yip of excitement and launched himself at her.

Thank you, Mac! The distraction gave her something safe to concentrate on and a chance to gather herself. When the mollified dog dashed off after a low-flying bird, she turned to find Zane sitting upright and removing his leg from the other bench.

"Leave it there," she said quickly. His smile was slightly guarded, but a smile all the same. The first all week, she decided, feeling irrationally pleased.

"I was making space for you. If you act nice, maybe sit awhile, it'll reassure your neighbour."

Julia spun around toward Mrs. H.'s yard, and Zane chuckled.

"Yeah, that's the one. She's been peering through the undergrowth at me for the last hour."

Feeling more than a little contrite, Julia sat. She should have told her neighbours about Zane moving in. She'd put it off because…well, because it was easier.

"How was your day?" he asked, much the same as every other evening this week. Yet today he'd smiled. Today he had invited her to sit, and he was watching her instead of turning away.

So today she didn't say, "Fine," and leave it there. She talked, inanely, at length, about her shift at the department store customer service desk. "And how about you?" she countered when she'd exhausted her stock of anecdotes.

"Big day. Saw the physio *and* took Mac for a walk."

He stretched his leg out in front, making himself comfortable, and she studied the thigh-to-ankle brace he'd been wearing ever since she picked him up from Gav and Lisa's. "How long do you have to wear that thing?"

"Another four weeks."

"Is it for protection? Support?"

"Mostly protection. It restricts movement, stops me bending the knee too far."

"Which would be bad?"

"Precisely."

Encouraged by his chattiness—heck, he'd said more words in the last minute than in the previous five days—she studied the leg more openly. Gave in to the curiosity she'd previously squelched. "What did they do exactly, when they operated?"

"Operation stories are dull."

"Duller than my Gracey's stories?"

He laughed, and the rich sound spread through her like warmed honey. Perhaps if he laughed more often she would develop some sort of immunity. Or perhaps not. Then he cocked his head to one side and considered her narrowly, and a frisson of alarm whispered around the edges of her mellow mood. He patted the seat beside him. "Come sit over here."

"Why?"

"I need an exposed knee for demonstration purposes." He indicated his, one hidden beneath denim, the other under the brace. "Mine aren't."

Julia hesitated.

"You want to know how this operation went down or not?"

With a put-upon sigh, she moved over to the other bench.

"Knee?"

She rolled her eyes. But when he reached toward her skirt, she hastily complied, lifting it just enough to uncover one knee.

"Okay. Here comes the anatomy lesson. I snapped the anterior cruciate ligament, which connects here to here."

He illustrated by drawing an imaginary line from her shinbone past her knee to the edge of her skirt. It was a chaste demonstration, nothing untoward. Yet Julia felt heat flood her skin, felt a soft yielding in her bones. She shifted uneasily, then covered the action by turning slightly toward him. The side benefit: it removed her from his reach. "How did they fix it?"

"In simple terms, by drilling a hole in each of those bones and threading a piece of replacement ligament from one to the other, grafting it at each end and sealing the whole thing with screws."

"Ouch."

"I didn't feel a thing."

Julia did. She tucked her feet up under her, hugging them close. "Do you have to wear the brace all the time?"

"Pretty much."

"When you sleep?"

"Yep."

"What about when you shower?"

He grinned. "Haven't you been wondering about all the plastic wrap in the garbage?"

"You wrap it all up? How on earth do you manage that?"

"With difficulty."

"You *could* ask for help."

Beside her, she felt him still. "You're kidding, right?"

Was she? The brace covered his whole leg, all the way up to the roughly hacked-off leg of his jeans. Except in the bathroom there would be no jeans. He would be naked.

And she was pretty sure her hands wouldn't be steady. Her vision turned a little blurry. She blew out a hot breath and tried to recall the point she'd been trying to make.

"Maybe the wrapping would be...awkward...but I could help with other things. For example, I could have hemmed your jeans where you cut them off."

"I like them this way."

Strike one. "I assume you have exercises. I could help with those."

"I manage on my own."

Strike two. "I know you can't drive, so if there's any time you need a lift, just ask."

"Thanks, but the exercise is good for me."

Struck out. Julia shook her head with exasperation. "Lisa warned me."

"You've been talking to Lisa about me?"

She shifted uneasily under his accusing gaze. "Only the day I picked you up. We talked a bit while we made lunch."

"What, exactly, did she warn you about?"

"She said you were too stubborn and independent to accept her help."

"You don't think she was busy enough without running around after me?"

"She *wanted* to help you. She felt guilty about you hurting your leg because of Jay."

"*She* felt guilty? Jay wouldn't have been up the damn tree if he hadn't heard me say it was built for climbing."

"That doesn't make it your fault," she said gently.

"He was in my care, Julia. I shouldn't have taken my eyes off him. Not for a second."

Oh, Zane. Everything about his tense posture, his bitter tone, the self-disgust in his eyes, called to her. Irresistibly.

She reached out, put a hand on his shoulder, and felt him stiffen reflexively.

"Don't look at me like that. I don't want your pity."

His voice was as sharp as his quicksilver eyes, and Julia quickly withdrew her hand. "That wasn't my intention."

"No? Then why did you touch me? Why are you so keen on helping me?"

"To show I care, that's all."

"No ulterior motive?"

Ulterior motive? Julia couldn't stop the guilty flare of colour, or the instinctive movement, hand to belly. Could he have guessed? No. She rejected the thought immediately. He hadn't been questioning her reason for coming to collect him, for having him in her home. Only her reason for touching him. "It was meant as comfort. I'm sorry."

"Hell, Julia, if you want to touch me—*anywhere*—I'm not about to object. Just don't expect me to be comforted. And don't go apologizing."

"Do you mean...?"

"...that I want you to touch me?" His eyes met hers, their message hot and direct. Julia felt her heart begin to pound heavily. "That I lie in bed every night with only a wall separating us, thinking about you touching me?"

Julia swallowed. Moistened her dry lips. "I didn't know. You haven't let on."

"You think I should have knocked on the wall?"

"What about your...injury?"

"It's my knee that's busted. Everything else is working just fine."

She resisted the urge to check that out. Barely. But while heat surged through her veins, while her heart screamed, *Yes! He still feels it too!* her head cautioned her to go slowly. Things could get very complicated in the next few days. "I don't think it would be a good idea."

"It was never a good idea, Julia. You and me. That didn't stop us the last time."

"There are other things to consider now. Your knee, the fact we're sharing a house."

He expelled a short, harsh laugh. "Hey, you can just say you're not interested."

If only it were that easy. "It's not that. It's just…complicated." She met his unfathomable gaze, begged him to understand. She didn't mean no, full stop. She meant yes, but later. And suddenly it seemed very important that she get from now to later as quickly as possible. She squared her shoulders. "I have to go over to Cliffton before the shops close. How about I bring home some takeaway?"

He looked right into her eyes for a long second before he seemed to gather himself. "Don't bother with dinner for me. I'll get something downtown."

"You're going out?"

"It's time I saw Bill about moving."

Her heart leap-frogged. "You don't have to do that."

"Yeah. I do."

Arguing was pointless—she could tell by his intractable expression. "Okay, but I'd really appreciate it if you held fire for a few days."

"Why?"

She crossed her fingers and sucked in a deep breath. "I was relying on your help with this fence. I have all day off tomorrow, and I'd hoped to get a decent start." Then, because his eyes seemed to be narrowing in a suspicious way, she grabbed her discarded bag, found the brochures and set them down between them on the bench. "Perhaps you could have a look at these and tell me what you think.''

"Now?"

"While I'm over in Cliffton."

She didn't wait for his answer. She just stood, then walked away. And she silently prayed that he would still be here when she returned.

The day had been going so well. After a week akin to torture, his knee had finally turned the corner. He'd been feeling so pleased with himself that even the neighbour's scrutiny hadn't bothered him. Julia's had. It had bothered his hormones in the most elemental of ways, and he hadn't been able to help himself. He'd asked her to sit. He'd encouraged her to talk. Hell, he'd even thought up a way to touch her without getting himself slapped.

Then came the shower business. Imagining her kneeling in front of him, slowly wrapping his leg all the way up to his groin, feeling the soft brush of her knuckles....

In the blink of a dark-lashed, hazel eye, he'd turned steel-hard. Ironic, really, how the talk of winding soft plastic wrap had led to the unraveling of the iron will he'd worked so hard to develop this past week.

This past *eight* weeks.

Still, he might have been able to apply the brakes if she hadn't put her hand on him. If she hadn't sat there looking at him with that hazy indecision clouding her eyes. As if she wanted him but something was holding her back. "Complications," she'd said. Perhaps she was worried over what people such as her neighbour would think. A one-night stand with someone like him was one thing, an ongoing affair another beast altogether.

He collected his crutches and settled them into his armpits. Plenty's only motel stood on the edge of town, a real haul from Bower Street, but that was the direction he pointed himself. Better to be independent than to expect help from either Bill or Julia. Plus, getting himself between the motel and her place over the next couple of days, while he built this fence, might convert about eight weeks' worth of sexual tension into sweat.

Might stop his self-control slipping its clutch again.

He picked up another gear, swinging the crutches in a smooth, even rhythm that saw the pavement fly under him in a grey blur of motion. He didn't slacken stride once, and it was only after he'd limped into the coolness of the motel reception area that he realized how hard he'd pushed himself. Sweat ran freely, and he grabbed the bottom edge of his shirt to mop at his face. Swore a blue streak when he put too much weight on his knee.

Recovered to find he wasn't alone.

The middle-aged woman behind the desk eyed him with a mixture of distaste and horror, and he knew he'd made a critical error in judgement, coming here dressed like this, looking like this. He simply hadn't been thinking beyond escape.

"How may I help you?" the woman asked. Zane knew the only place she wanted to help him was out the door.

"I need a room for at least two weeks, maybe longer."

"I'm sorry, but we're fully booked."

"Every room?" He glanced at the registration book still firmly closed beneath her hands. "Shouldn't you check?"

"I do all the bookings, and I know we don't have a room for you."

"Look, lady, my money's worth the same as anyone else's." He extracted his wallet from his hip pocket and grabbed a stack of notes. "I'll pay whatever it takes."

Her nose twitched with distaste. Or suspicion. "Have you tried the hotel? I believe their rooms are well priced."

"They're also up about thirty stairs." He lifted one of his crutches to illustrate his point, but she remained visibly unmoved. Although when he leaned closer to pick up a business card, she took a quick step backward. That rubbed the wrong end of his temper. He tapped a finger against the card. "Maybe you should check with the manager— Mr. Grainger, is it?"

"I'm *Mrs.* Grainger and I speak for my husband. We can't help you. Is that all?"

"You heard me the first time," Bill drawled. "I can't look after you. You're better off where you are."

A red haze crossed his vision, and Zane closed his eyes. "I don't expect you to look after me. I'm only asking for a patch of floor to put a mattress."

Bill snorted. "You'd be a pain in the neck, sitting around here belly-aching about nothing to fill your time."

Man, he hated having to beg. To plead. "I'm asking a favor here. I'm not comfortable where I am. It's like a doll's house."

"This is hardly the Hilton."

"Come on, man, it's driving me crazy living there."

Bill's wizened face cracked into a sly grin. "Girl's getting to you, isn't she? And you can't do a thing about it."

He ignored that. "You gonna give me a break?"

"I'll give you a lift back."

Zane ground his teeth. "Don't bother. I'm not a total invalid."

Zane didn't think things could get any worse, but that was before he tackled the six blocks to Julia's as if they were an Olympic sprint final. Before he needed to stop and catch his breath ten meters from the finish line. No medal for you, bud, he decided with a twist of dry humor. He propped his tired body against a sturdy fence.

"What are you doing there?" The stern voice came from the yard behind him. "Shoo, or I'll call the police."

Zane straightened from his perch. It was the neighbour, the one who'd been watching him earlier, although he wasn't sure she recognized him in the tricky dusk light. Not until he turned. Then she did at least lower the gardening tool she'd been brandishing like a weapon.

He leaned his weight on one crutch and extended a hand. "I should have introduced myself this afternoon. I'm Zane O'Sullivan, Kree's brother. I'm staying with Julia."

"I know who you are." She ignored his hand. "How long are you staying?"

The look on her face was a carbon copy of the motel manager's. Zane got the message, loud and clear.

"No longer than I can help," he told her with admirable restraint.

He felt her watch him every step of the way into Julia's yard—the perfect end to a hellish couple of hours that had only served to confirm what he'd known all along. The good townspeople of Plenty had long memories, and when it came to Zane O'Sullivan, not one of those memories was good.

Nine

Julia pressed a hand to her mouth to muffle her spontaneous squeal of joy, but she couldn't squelch the wide grin
that threatened to split her face from ear to ear.

She stared at the prophetic little stick until it turned
blurry around the edges. Then in the middle. Then, when
she couldn't see anything through her tears, when her wob-
bly legs refused to support her, she sat. Sniffling like a
child, beaming like an idiot, she didn't care that she was
sitting on cold bathroom tiles. She touched a trembling
hand to her still-flat stomach with awed reverence.

Inside her, a baby grew. Her baby. Hers and Zane's.
Despite her suspicions, the possibility had seemed too remote to allow herself to believe, or to succumb to the
myriad questions now tumbling through her mind. Including the most insistent.

How could this be so?

Every time he'd used protection. Even when he sank

into her body in sleep-dazed mindlessness, he'd withdrawn almost immediately. One of the condoms mustn't have done its job. It was the only explanation, and the most ironic.

All those years with Paul, all her wishing that one might fail, and she had never been so lucky. But then he had always been so meticulous, so measured, so...unlike Zane.

Wild, unpredictable, lightning-bolt Zane.

Oh, dear Lord, how would he take the news? All week she had struggled to suppress the memory of that morning on her veranda when he all but accused her of sleeping with him to fall pregnant.

Oh, dear Lord, how would she break the news?

The idea of hugging it to herself, of stealing some time to simply savor the joy, played a seductive tune around the edges of her conscience. Without very much effort she could even justify it.

You need time to allow this initial fizz to settle, time to consider all the implications. Time to carefully select the right words.

"No." She sat up straight. "You have to tell him. *Now,* if not sooner."

Except there'd been no sign of him when she'd returned from Cliffton, and the house seemed ominously quiet. In his own words he'd had a big day, so he might be in his room resting. Or he might have packed up and left, despite her plea. Despite her calling in at Bill's and enlisting his help. Perhaps she should just go and knock on his bedroom door. That seemed like the logical thing to do, but Julia hesitated.

She couldn't forget the way he'd looked at her in the garden this afternoon. Couldn't forget the searing impact of his words. *I lie in bed every night with only a wall separating us, thinking about you touching me.* If she knocked on his door, if she found him there in that bed, she wouldn't be able to think of anything but touching him. She wouldn't be able to concentrate, and oh, how she needed every one of her wits for this conversation.

Sitting there on the floor stewing over it wasn't helping. With a ragged sigh, she pulled herself up from the floor and rubbed some circulation into her numb behind.

Outside his door she paused, waited, heard nothing. As she made her way to her own room she tried not to feel too relieved about the reprieve, or to contemplate the possibility that she might have to go searching for him in the morning.

She didn't expect to sleep much, and she didn't. Yet Julia rose with more energy than she'd felt for months. Oh, she didn't fool herself that the juices coursing through her system derived from anything other than pure nerves, but after she'd defrosted the refrigerator, hung three loads of washing and scrubbed the bathroom until the tiles gleamed, she was still jumping.

And she was still alone.

She thought about walking Mac, rejected it. Thought about calling in at Bill's and rejected that thought, as well. But she walked, nonetheless, with long, invigorating strides, for mile after mile. Strangely, the activity seemed to feed her strength rather than sap it—or perhaps that was due to her increasingly resolute frame of mind.

In the long run Zane's reaction didn't matter. Oh, she knew his negative response would have the power to hurt her very badly, but, if necessary, she would do this alone. *Could* do this alone. She would be the best mother she could be, with or without Zane at her side.

Lost in thought, she would have walked right past her gate but for the sound of the screen door clicking shut.

Her stomach lurched with a sick mix of nerves and dread as she swung around. A man loped down the path and through the front gate, then stopped dead in his tracks.

"Tim." Not the man she'd been expecting to see. "What are you doing here?"

"Hoping I might bump into you, actually."

With a sinking heart, she noticed how pleased he looked to see her. She shouldn't have gone out with him, shouldn't have let him kiss her, and definitely shouldn't have let him think he could call her again. All because she'd been too weak to tell him it wouldn't work. That she'd felt nothing.

"I tried calling last night and earlier this morning but only got your machine. I know it's a bit last minute, but a few of us are taking a hike through the Tibba and I hoped you might join me...us...no, *me*." He laughed self-consciously and tucked his hands into the pockets of his cords. "Your flatmate said he didn't know when you'd be back. Talk about good timing."

Julia felt an insane desire to laugh. Good timing? Could he have chosen a worse day? "I'm sorry, Tim, but I have plans."

"Maybe another time? With more notice?"

"I don't think—" Phew, this was difficult. Involuntarily, her gaze flicked to the shadowy veranda. Zane was there, watching. Listening? She seemed to be saying this a lot lately, but again it was apt. "I don't think that's a good idea."

Colour bled into Tim's face as he followed the direction of her gaze. She'd forgotten he was an accountant, quick to add two and two. "I'm sorry. I didn't realize. Chantal led me to believe you were...unattached."

Unattached? Perhaps unencumbered would have been a better choice of adjective. She blew out a puff of breath.

"Yes, well, that's my fault. Chantal didn't know the situation had...changed. I'm sorry, Tim, I truly am."

He should make himself scarce. Now, while she was waving Volvo Man, Mark II, goodbye. But Zane couldn't bring himself to move any more than he could stop himself grinding gears over her visitor. What was it with her and men who drove Volvos? Apart from the fact that they smelled like money instead of sweat and hard work. Not that it was any of his business. He should just take himself inside or out back, anywhere he wasn't tempted to start interrogating her. Except she was coming up the path, and the first question was already there. On his tongue. "Friend of yours?"

She gave a slight shrug. "We went out once."

"And he wants to take you out again." It was a statement, not a question. Of course he would want to take her out again. What man wouldn't?

"A group's going hiking, and he asked me to join them."

"And?"

She leaned back against a solid veranda post and looked right at him. "I told him I had other plans."

For a moment he became tangled in the intricate web of her eyes, in the concept that she'd sent Volvo Man on his way because her plans all involved hot, horizontal and him. And then he remembered. "The fence."

"There is that." She looked down at her feet, and Zane followed her gaze. Watched her cross one slender ankle over the other, then back again. Nervously? "To be honest, the fence was an excuse of sorts to keep you here."

His gaze rocketed to her face; his body rocketed to attention. She wanted to keep him here.... "Because?"

"So I can talk to you."

"About what I said yesterday afternoon?"

"Not really…or perhaps a little." She blew out a breath that seemed to catch in the middle. It definitely caught at Zane, caught and tugged everything at least six holes tighter. "I did have an ulterior motive in wanting you here."

Blood surged through his veins. Euphoria surged through his brain. *She wanted him. Here.* Forget semantics, forget willpower, forget complications. Forget the bed with sheets still tangled from another sleepless night. Another night of wanting, of not having….

He crossed the three steps separating them in two. Barely caught the surprised rounding of her eyes, the impulsive touch of tongue to bottom lip, before he pressed her back against the post. Hard body perfectly aligned with soft. Then his hands were buried in her hair and his mouth was sucking up her gasp of surprise, and he was kissing her, tasting her, lapping up her essence. How had he lived eight weeks without it?

He tore his mouth away, but not his body. "If I've got your ulterior motive wrong, you better speak up now."

Hips pressed hard against hers, he felt her body's soft yielding, then the touch of her hand on his cheek. He lifted his head, looked down into her troubled hazel eyes, and in the periphery of his awareness heard another vehicle slow and brake. "If that's another Volvo, I won't be responsible for my actions."

A car door slammed, and she let go a husky laugh. "Do you suppose if I hide here behind you, whoever it is might just go away?"

Zane rested his chin on top of her head and caught a glimpse of *whoever* it is before he ducked down to open the back door of his Land Rover. "You could and he might, but I think you'd be sorry later." Reluctantly, he unsnagged her fingers from his shirtfront and stepped back. "It's your brother."

Blinking slowly, she straightened, moistened her mouth and turned. A second later she was hurtling down the path, laughing and talking and throwing herself into Mitch's arms—not an easy task when Mitch's arms were already full of a wriggling, squealing child.

Then Mitch dropped an affectionate kiss on the top of her head, and Zane felt a solid punch to the solar plexus. It left him breathless, off-balance, disturbed, and he turned away abruptly. Left them to their touching family reunion. But long after he closed the door at his back he could still hear her laughter, could still see the look of delight on the kid's face as he fastened his arms around her neck. Could still feel an unaccountable emptiness where he'd felt that punch of reaction.

Somewhere around midnight the previous night he'd given up trying to sleep. By the light of a three-quarter moon he'd prowled the yard, tossed sticks for Mac, and then drawn up a mental plan for the fence. Julia's approval was pending, but whatever her final decision on materials, the fence needed posts. Posts needed holes. And the prospect of attacking raw earth with a sharp-edged steel implement fit his current mood like a glove.

Fifteen minutes later he threw down the shovel in frustration. His injured knee screamed, *No more.* He needed a post-hole digger. He needed Julia to go fetch it. He was leaning on the shovel, the notion of asking for help stuck tight in his craw, when the back door crashed open to expel a fair-haired boy like a shot from a pistol.

The pocket dynamo made a beeline for Mac, and Zane barely had time to form the association—small unknowing child, large exuberant dog—before the two came together in a rolling, squealing, barking tumble of legs and arms and fur. Zane's heart stuttered with alarm. He rushed toward them, whistling at Mac, who paid him no heed. It took another slow angsty second before he remembered both dog and kid belonged to Mitch. And the kid's only danger lay in being licked to death.

He collapsed onto the garden bench. Closed his eyes. Adrenaline still coursed through his body. And his bloody knee was throbbing again. It was time he started looking after it better or he would end up back in the hospital. He would be stuck here forever recuperating. Forever wanting Julia, continually being interrupted, eternally hard and frustrated.

Something bumped into his good leg and he opened his eyes to find the boy staring up at him with wide solemn eyes. They were so like Julia's he could only stare back. Couldn't think of a damn thing to say.

"Is your leg broke?"

Zane cleared his throat. "You might say that."

"What broke it?"

"I fell out of a tree."

The kid's brow puckered. "What was you doing in a tree?"

Zane didn't think he should mention the real reason. He was still trying to think of an alternate when he heard the back door open and close. He knew it was Julia without looking.

"I see you two have met."

"Not formally."

"*He* fell out of a tree. Was it that tree?" One pudgy finger pointed at the big cedar in the corner.

"*He* is Zane, and I won't let *him* climb my tree, either."

"Damn blast."

"Joshua Goodwin! Where did you hear that?"

"Daddy said it." The kid—Joshua—smiled unapologetically. "Does your leg hurt?"

"All the time," Julia answered for him. "Now, how about we take Mac for a walk?"

"You wanna come, too?" he asked Zane.

"Love to, but my leg needs rest." He glanced at Julia. "Where's Mitch?"

"Hey, Joshua. You remember where we keep Mac's leash?" she called brightly. Only when the kid was out of earshot did she turn troubled eyes on him. "Mitch had to go. Joshua is staying with us for a little while."

"Us?"

Maybe it had been a slip of the tongue, but she didn't correct him, and he couldn't ignore the silent appeal shining in her eyes. Joshua was already racing across the lawn toward them, the leash dragging in his wake. Zane nodded his understanding. "You can explain later."

Later turned out to be *much* later. Between Joshua's needs and fence construction dramas—Zane insisted on digging, she insisted on hiring help, he insisted on laboring for the contractor—they had no time alone until after she'd fed, bathed and read Joshua to sleep. Then she collapsed onto the sofa.

"You want tea?" Zane asked from the kitchen.

She noticed he'd done all the cleaning up. She noticed nothing stood in the way of conversation, nothing but a need to gather her thoughts. In twelve hours she hadn't spared her pregnancy one of those scattered thoughts. Whenever her mind had wandered during the long day, it had been to revisit the staggering unexpectedness of that morning kiss. To wonder what might have happened if Mitch had happened along half an hour later.

"You still with us?"

Julia realized she'd been sitting there staring at him, his question unanswered. And she didn't need to answer, because he was sliding a cup of tea onto the table at her side. "Thanks, I absolutely need that. I'd forgotten how tiring a three-year-old can be."

"You should try twins."

The sofa dipped as he sat at the other end, and, tucking her feet up, Julia turned so she could face him. "Lisa said you coped amazingly well."

"Yeah, well, I did what I could."

Julia stifled a smile. Earlier he'd shrugged off her praise for his amazing job on the fence in similar fashion. And he looked so disarmingly gruff, so uncomfortable, so *cute*, she just wanted to crawl down there and hug him. Then he shifted position slightly, moving one arm to rest along the back of the sofa, and the overhead light caught the shifting curve of muscle in his upper arm. Heat, instant and unexpected, whipped through her body.

No. Zane O'Sullivan wasn't cute. He was downright dangerous.

"So what's the story with Mitch?"

Julia blinked. Mitch. What *was* the story with Mitch? She cleared her throat. "Annabel's left him."

Surprise whistled softly through his teeth. "Serious or a spat?"

"Not a spat, that's for sure. She's been on a long shoot in Europe, and she just rang to say she's not coming back."

His pause seemed deliberate, measured. The weight of his gaze felt the same. "Another man?"

"Mitch didn't say, but I guess it's possible. I mean, she's a mother as well as a wife, so she wouldn't just do this on a whim, not with Joshua to consider. Which is why

Mitch wanted to get on the first plane he could, to go over there and talk to her.''

He cocked his head in the direction of the room where Joshua slept. "So he's here for a while?"

"Three or four days. Mum and Dad are coming home as soon as they can get flights. They'll take him back to Sydney and look after him in his own home, where he's less likely to fret.'' She sipped at her tea and tried not to start fretting for him. Failed miserably. "I keep wondering when he'll start asking questions. Usually he only stays overnight, two at most. When Mitch is gone longer, he'll want to know why, and I can't lie to him. What do I say? How can I explain?"

"You don't have to explain anything. He's only three."

"Yes, but—"

"Yes, but nothing. Stop borrowing trouble, Julia. You'll handle it when you have to, the same calm, competent way you handle everything.''

"You think so?" She held out a hand so he could see the tremor. "This doesn't look calm and competent to me.''

In perfect illustration, her voice quavered and cracked on the last syllable. The threat of tears tickled the back of her throat, and she would have rushed to her feet, got out of the room before they overflowed, if he hadn't reached out and trapped her tremulous hand in his. Forced her to look at him. "You want to talk about what's really bothering you?"

"Mitch and Annabel and Josh are what's bothering me!"

His thumb stroked across her wrist with steady reassurance. "You're not finding this situation a bit déjà vu?"

Perplexed, she shook her head.

"I'm talking about *your* marriage, Julia. When your husband left you."

She blinked in surprise. The parallel hadn't even registered. If there was a parallel. "Paul didn't just leave, not like Annabel. It was more a…mutual decision."

"Wasn't there another woman?"

"Yes, but he told me about her. We talked, and we tried to work things out, but he'd fallen in love with her. I knew that." She shrugged matter-of-factly. "I couldn't stay in a marriage like that."

"What if there'd been a child?"

It was the perfect opening. He was still holding her hand, still looking at her with that seductive mix of concern and comfort. All she had to do was say, *There* is *a child, Zane. Our child.* But, God help her, she couldn't do it. Not yet, not without knowing more.

"Do you think a child needs two parents?" she blurted.

"Is this a general question, or are you talking specifics?"

Julia's heart somersaulted and lodged in her throat.

"Because if you're talking about Joshua, who am I to say? He seems happy, well adjusted, like his parents are doing their job. In which case he's better off with both."

Profound relief washed through her. He'd been talking about Joshua; he hadn't looked into her eyes and read her secret. And now he wasn't looking into her eyes at all. He seemed distracted, far away, perhaps years away. Was he thinking about *his* parents, about *those* specifics?

Bringing up his past was risky, but she had to know which scars had healed and which still lay open to further hurt. And why, eight weeks before, he'd said marriage was low on his priority list.

"There are plenty of circumstances when a child is better off with only one parent, though," she said carefully.

Something flashed across the surface of his eyes, something cold and bleak, and for a second Julia regretted starting this, but only for a scant second. She had to know.

"What about you, Zane? When did your parents split up?"

"They didn't so much split up as tear themselves apart. My father was a real no-hoper, an alcoholic. Never kept a job longer than a month. If my mother had been stronger, she'd have kicked him out long before—" He stopped abruptly. Shook his head. "You don't want to hear about my sorry family."

Oh, but she did. She looked into his cold, closed expression, and she felt a stab of longing so sharp she swore it drew blood. She twisted her hand in his, squeezed his fingers. "Tell me. I absolutely want to know."

He stared at her a moment, as if judging her sincerity or her reason for wanting to know. When he pulled his hand free of hers, she held her breath and willed him not to cut her off completely. His Adam's apple dipped as if he were clearing his throat, and she clasped her hands tightly together. *Talk to me, Zane. Please.*

"There's not a lot to tell. Eventually he got caught stealing, and he died in a prison fight." He shrugged, but she knew it was a feigned negligence. "A few weeks afterward we landed here. In the town of Plenty."

His tone mocked the town's name, and she recalled the time he'd added his editorial comment to the town's Welcome sign. Unfortunately his opinion on what the town offered plenty of didn't exactly gel with the city council's. He would likely have ended up charged with vandalism if Bill hadn't stepped in and offered him a chance to pay off the damage.

"You hated the place, didn't you?"

"I hated how it made me feel." He studied his hands

for a long silent moment, then let go his breath sharply. "You ever see that movie *Pleasantville?* Where the only road out of town circles around and comes back in the other side? That was my worst nightmare, being trapped in this town."

"And that's why you left."

"Just as soon as I finished my apprenticeship."

"Not because of Claire Heaslip?" she asked compulsively.

"Claire?" He glanced up, his eyes flat and hard. "I guess you heard the rumors."

"Yes, but gossip isn't always accurate."

"The bit about her using me for a trip on the wild side, that's accurate, but as for her allegations... She wasn't pregnant, at least not by me. That's not why she left town, and not why I left, either."

That was worse than the gossip she'd heard. A cold sense of misgiving washed over Julia. A supposed good girl from the rich end of town had used him for sex, had started pregnancy rumors. No wonder he looked so bitter now, remembering. No wonder he had sounded so bitter that morning on her veranda.

"I left because I couldn't wait to get out of this place. I was ashamed of the hovel we lived in. I couldn't invite my friends around, and I hated going to their places, seeing what we didn't have."

Julia ached to comfort him, to touch him in some way, but she recalled how he'd accused her of touching him in pity, and she knew that was the last thing he needed now.

"I hated who I was, I hated my parents for making me who I was, and I hated the town for making me realize everything I wasn't. Everything I could never be."

"That's one way of looking at it," she said slowly.

"There's another?"

Ignoring the biting edge to his voice, she tilted her head consideringly. "Bill says you're a damn fine mechanic. Almost as good as him."

"I was better than him ten years ago!"

"Because he taught you everything he knows?"

He snorted disparagingly. "Because I questioned everything he didn't know."

"So, Mr. Hotshot Mechanic, don't you think you should be thanking your parents and this town and Bill? Seems to me they gave you the incentive to prove them wrong."

"This town doesn't see me as anything but a troublemaker. Haven't you heard that on the grapevine?"

"As I said before, Plenty gossip is rarely accurate."

He expelled a rough-sounding laugh, shook his head. "You're really something, aren't you?"

"Well, yes, but I'm not sure what."

Her dry response, the accompanying smile, were meant to lighten the mood, but somehow she became snagged in the lure of his answering smile, in the light of speculation in his eyes. In the strange charge in the atmosphere between them—strange because it transcended the physical, because it pulsed between them in some deeper dimension.

She knew he felt it, too.... He felt it, and it disturbed him. He looked away, studied his hands again, and a wry smile kicked up one corner of his mouth. "You know, back in high school, whenever I thought of what I didn't have, it was Mitch Goodwin I was looking at. I wanted to be him. I wanted his life."

"You don't want to be Mitch now. He's devastated." Julia recalled the pain in her brother's eyes, his sense of helplessness, of bewilderment. "I wish there was something I could do, some way of easing his pain. I feel so ineffectual."

"Taking Joshua seems pretty effectual to me."

She made a soft scoffing noise. "It's a great big nothing."

"You think Mitch wants to be worrying about Joshua when he's on the other side of the world talking some sense into his wife? You think he isn't grateful as all hell to have a safe place to leave his kid? To know he's happy?"

"I hadn't thought of it like that." She met the directness of his gaze, felt some of its steady strength seep into her, comforting her as effortlessly as his words. "Now all I have to do is work out some way to keep my job while providing that safe, happy, child care."

"Can't you take a sickie?" He must have seen the horrified look on her face, because he smiled wryly. "No, of course not."

"I'll work something out." Except finding someone to cover on such short notice would be a nightmare.

"I could look after him while you go in and see your boss, if that helps any."

Julia shook her head. "I can't do that."

"Can't or won't?"

"Of course I can." She stared at him, remembering his guilt over failing with Jay, and she knew this mattered. That her trust mattered. "Perhaps if you'd just take him in the morning, until I can go in and sort out something for my other shifts. I hate leaving them in the lurch. Would that be okay with you?"

"No sweat."

"You're a life-saver." She smiled her gratitude. "Seems like I'll owe you another drink."

"You never bought me the first two."

"Yes, well, I seem to recall being sidetracked."

In two short sentences the mood changed substance, became a thing of fire and electricity.

"It's been a long day," he said slowly. "I don't think we should go any further down this road."

Their eyes met, and memories flickered, flared, flamed into life. That morning, their interrupted kiss, the pressure of his body, hard and ready.

Did she want to travel that road? *Oh, yes, most definitely.* But not until she'd cleared every one of the obstacles, and that was a huge task of road-clearing to be starting tonight.

So when he took her by the hands, pulled her to her feet and pressed a chaste kiss to her forehead, she didn't resist. When he turned her firmly in the direction of her bedroom, she kept on walking.

Somehow it just seemed easier.

Ten

He was being watched by the dragon lady in number sixteen again, although watched wasn't the right word when it felt more like surveillance. Normally she would have driven him nuts hours ago, but this morning his mood was too laid back. Playing with trucks in the sandpit had that effect on him. His whole body felt looser, as though it had kicked back a few cogs and was running on the sweetest timing.

With a suddenness Zane was almost getting used to, Josh abandoned his Tonka truck and clambered to his feet. "Can we walk Mac now?"

"Good a time as any, bud." Zane stretched and had to bite back a curse. He hadn't thought about sand inside his brace when he signed on at Josh's construction site. "How 'bout you get his leash while I clean out this bi—" He caught himself in time. "This big old brace?"

The kid was already steaming away to fetch the leash,

his sturdy legs pumping like pistons. Zane grinned and shook his head. Yep, his mood was unusually sunny when even sand abrasion couldn't sour it. Of course, it was impossible to be anything but cheerful around Josh—the kid was a three-foot beam of pure sunshine—but he would be fooling himself if he didn't acknowledge the real reason.

Julia. He felt as if she'd handed him some rare gift last night, yet he couldn't even begin to fathom all its facets. There'd been the fact that she trusted him with Joshua, no hesitation, no provisos. And before that, the way she'd listened to his story as though she really needed to hear it, as though she wanted to figure out its significance. As though it mattered. Then she'd blown him away with that strange insight into what Plenty had done for him.

Needless to say, she'd blown him away all over again with her unspoken invitation...the one he had gently rejected. There had been a shadow darkening her eyes—a worry, a reservation, a concern. It could have been because of Mitch and the day's high emotion, or it could have arisen from his story. Whatever the reason, it had held him back when her body gravitated toward his. Told him to kiss her on the brow instead of the mouth. He hadn't stopped to analyse the reason, but he'd known that the next time he pressed himself into her soft body, there would be no shadows in her eyes.

Until then, he would keep on howling.

The neighbour—Mrs. H., Julia called her—was watering her front yard when they returned from their walk. He'd abandoned his crutches, and it felt damn good to be on his own two feet again.

"Lovely day for gardening," he suggested.

She glared at him a second before her acerbic eyes

dropped to Josh. And instantly warmed. "Hello, young man. Are you visiting with your auntie Julia?"

"What's an arnty?"

The kid's question—like its two hundred odd predecessors—was directed at Zane, but Dragon Lady answered. "That means Julia is your father's sister. I saw you were visiting, and I made a batch of those cookies you love."

"The ones with hun'reds and fousands?"

She beamed with delight. "Yes, and if you send your auntie over later, she can collect them."

"Can Zane c'lect 'em now?"

Mrs. H.'s affectionate laughter evaporated as she glanced from Josh to Zane. He crossed his arms and smiled benignly. The perfect mimic, Josh crossed his arms and smiled, too, although his was definitely a winner. That and the magic word he suddenly remembered. "I forgot to say please."

"Well, in that case…"

When she hurried off inside, Zane high-fived Josh. "Good cookies, huh?"

"Uh-huh."

Removing that tub of cookies from her reluctant hands shouldn't have felt so sweet, Zane told himself as he demolished his third. But he couldn't prevent his grin from widening when he recalled the look on her face as she sternly informed him, "They're for Joshua, you hear?"

Now Josh put a chubby hand on his shoulder and peered into his face. "What you wanna do now, Zane?"

He considered the possibilities. Cookies aside, it was nearing lunchtime. Julia's knock-off time. "How about lunch in the park?"

"The one wiff ducks?"

"That's the one."

"Can Julia come, too?"

Zane grinned. "We can always ask."

Julia felt the sharp nudge of an elbow in her side, heard Kerrie's, "Oh, wow, *serious* babe alert," and looked up. Not to check out another of Kerrie's infamous "babe alerts," but to suggest that her workmate return her focus to the inventory checklist.

Then her attention was snared by the sight coming through the furnishings department. A tall man with tawny blond hair ruffled all out of shape by the fingers that gripped it. They belonged to the small boy with mussy blond hair riding on the man's broad shoulders. Two pairs of eyes scanned the floor with equal thoroughness.

The father-son imagery curled into her senses and made itself at home. Oh, yes, *this* was what she wanted. This man. Their child. The whole family deal.

The knowledge didn't strike her like a thunderbolt, didn't knock the breath from her lungs or the strength from her legs. It rippled through her like liquid sunshine and pooled somewhere near her heart. She loved him. Absolutely, unreservedly, forever-and-a-day-ly.

While she was still absorbing the significance of that acknowledgement, Joshua spotted her. He pointed and bounced and, judging by the grimace on Zane's face, tightened his hair-hold with the other hand. Julia was smiling all over her face before their gazes met and held, and she felt such a giddy rush of hope and joy and love that she laughed out loud.

Kerrie nudged her again and suggested *she* stop gawking and get back to work, but Julia ignored her. They were only ten feet away and closing fast, and she felt a sudden attack of shyness. A certainty that everything she felt was right there on her face, that he would take one look and decide to bolt. With infinite care, as if it were something incredibly fragile, she put down her pen. Then looked up into eyes the clear grey of spring rain.

"Hi."

"Hi." She mimicked his greeting, although she wasn't sure how. Then Joshua was chattering about how they'd come to take her to the park to feed ducks, and to hurry, because the bread would be stale, until finally he stopped to take a breath.

"So," Zane said slowly. "You want to come to the park with us?"

She thought there might be a challenge in his eyes, but she hadn't a clue what it meant. All she knew was if he continued to look at her that way, she would crawl over glass to get to the park. Although she didn't think she would tell him that quite yet—not until she'd told him something much more daunting.

She felt that shadow cross her happiness like a storm cloud and attempted to chase it away with a smile. "Did you bring lunch for anyone other than the ducks? Because I'm starving."

Joshua rummaged in his jacket pocket and produced a severely crunched bag. "You can share wiff the ducks. They won't mind."

Zane and Julia bought sandwiches and ate them while Joshua wore himself out dashing between the play equipment and the lagoon that looped the park's southern boundary. Finally he collapsed against Zane's bad leg, and when she saw his involuntary wince, a bolt of contrition shot through her.

"Come over here, sport, and I'll piggyback you home."

"I'm not sport, I'm bud," he informed her without releasing his grip on Zane. "Will *you* piggyback me?"

"Shoulders?"

"'kay."

And before Julia could do more than open her mouth to object, Joshua had clambered aboard Zane's shoulders.

"Are you sure you can manage?" she worried.

"If bud here takes his hands off my eyes."

Joshua giggled. Julia rolled her eyes. And they started for home.

"What happened to your crutches?" she asked.

"Threw them away."

"Was that wise?"

He glanced down at her. "Worried I'll drop the kid?"

"No, I'm worried you'll hurt your knee again."

"Worrywort."

"Man."

He laughed out loud at her teasing choice of insult, and the husky-edged sound burrowed deep into her heart. She'd rarely seen him so relaxed, so quick to laugh. If only they could maintain this easy mood. If only...if only. She sighed heavily and felt the immediate touch of his gaze, and with a sinking heart she saw the question forming. But before he could ask it, Maisie Davis came out of the butcher shop and stopped to beam at them all. "Lovely day," she said.

"We've been to the park," Joshua supplied.

"I bet you had fun. Are you going home now?"

"No. We're going to Julia's place. Zane lives there, too, y'know."

Julia felt a burning heat in her ears and wished her hair wasn't tied back, but Maisie was too busy inspecting Zane to notice her discomfort. "You're young Kree's brother, aren't you? I do hope she comes back soon, because Tina doesn't know how to set my hair." She patted her tight curls. ''Well, you all have a nice day. I have to finish my shopping.''

In the next three blocks they exchanged pleasantries with at least six more townsfolk, all keen to chat with Joshua, to ask about Kree, to study Zane. She didn't dare look at him, to see how he was taking the unasked-for attention.

When they turned the last corner into a deserted Bower Street, she heard him blow out an incredulous kind of laugh. ''I've been out walking every day this last week, and you know, this is the first time anyone's passed the time of day.''

''Well, a child is a proven conversation starter,'' she said lightly. ''Or perhaps it's because you're not so fearsome when you're smiling.''

''Aren't you worried about your reputation?''

She glanced up, noticed he wasn't smiling now. ''You've been living in my house a week now. I think my reputation's pretty much besmirched.''

She'd intended to smile, to show her comment wasn't serious, but they were at the gate, going into her yard, and dread churned sickly in her stomach. Joshua would be asleep in five minutes, and then she couldn't put this off any longer. She had to tell him.

Josh insisted that Zane read him a story, and, despite Julia's protestations to give the man a break, he agreed. Two pages and the kid was out like a light, so it was no drama. He pulled the doona over the boy's far-flung limbs and quietly pulled the door closed behind him.

Music drifted out from the living room, one of those soft bluesy tunes she seemed to favor. The discordant clang of a saucepan placed her in the kitchen, and when he breathed more deeply, he caught the faint waft of something spicy.

She looked up when he wandered in. "I thought I'd get an early start on dinner, while he's taking a nap. Thank you for taking care of that."

"No sweat."

"You should go put your leg up."

"Yes, Mum."

Her spoon clattered from the pan, against the side of the stove and to the floor, and Julia just stood there staring at the tomato-coloured sauce splattered in its wake.

"Maybe you better come sit for a while, too," he suggested. She definitely looked as if she needed to sit down.

He bent to retrieve the spoon, but she waved him away with a muttered, "It's okay, just clumsy fingers. I'll be out in a minute."

As he grabbed a soft drink and headed out to his favorite sitting spot, he wondered about that bewildered look on her face, but he couldn't figure what had brought it on. Or if he'd imagined it.

He must have sat for a full twenty minutes, maybe more, listening to her music, stroking Mac's soft fur, before the back door clicked open and closed.

She'd changed from her work uniform into one of those soft dresses that hid yet hinted at what lay beneath, and she didn't come and sit with him.

Instead she moved about the yard on restless sneakered feet, bending to pull a stray weed here, plucking and discarding a dead flower there, grabbing a garden fork and scratching about in a bed. If he hadn't been enjoying the play of her dress around her curved derriere every time she bent or stretched, he would have called her over and made her park herself. If he hadn't been concentrating on the play of her dress, he mightn't have taken so long to notice the frown that furrowed her brow. The way her lips moved every so often, as if she were talking to herself. Or reciting something.

Something that bothered her.

Something she wasn't prepared to talk to him about.

He had no right to feel slighted, hurt, insulted. He had no right to expect she should want to share with him, but that didn't stop him feeling every one of those things in rapid-fire succession.

Then she put down the fork she'd been digging with and pushed her hands into the small of her back, as if to stretch tired muscles. Turning a fraction of a degree, the full extent of her stretch came into sudden stark silhouette, picked out by the brilliant rays of the afternoon sun. The upward tilt of her full breasts, the curve of her abdomen, the long lines of her legs, all clearly, breathtakingly, delineated.

For once the ache in his body wasn't solely in his jeans. Sure, it was centered there, but it seemed to grow to fill his gut, his chest, his whole being. To throb with a rich fullness that made him feel too big for his skin. Eyes closed, she twisted from the waist, enough that he could see her face and the small serene smile curving her lips. The way her other hand touched her belly almost protectively.

Zane's heart seemed to stop beating. It wasn't possible. He must be imagining things. He sat up suddenly, and she turned, must have caught the stunned expression on his face, and he felt as if he was watching a slow motion set of frames. Her hand fell away from her belly, the other from her back. She straightened, stiffened, and the stricken look in her eyes doused his doubts as surely as a bucket of cold water.

"When were you going to tell me?" he asked.

Slowly she approached, her steps as light and hesitant as her smile. "As soon as I worked out what to say, how to tell you."

"How about, 'I'm pregnant.' That would do the trick." She stopped dead in her tracks. So did her smile.

"How long have you known?" he asked.

"I did the test Friday night."

Zane blew out a breath. She'd known last night. She'd quizzed him about his attitude to marriage and kids and single parenthood *knowing* she was pregnant. She'd had every chance to tell him. Hell, if she'd really wanted to share, she'd had any number of opportunities.

"Is that why you went to Cliffton? To buy the kit?" He waited for her nod of acknowledgement. "Then you must have suspected?"

"Yes. But I wanted to be sure...before I said anything."

"And are you sure? Have you seen a doctor?"

He knew her answer before she shook her head. She wouldn't have seen a doctor here in Plenty for the same reason she didn't buy her test kit here in Plenty. Same reason she hadn't introduced him to her neighbours, or to any of the people who stopped to chat this afternoon. Same old story. Okay to sleep with, not to be seen with. Certainly not to be pregnant by.

"These tests are supposed to be as accurate as the doctor's." She rubbed her hands down the sides of her dress, nervously. "And I'm certain."

"Have you been sick?"

"Only tired. At first I thought that was because of work and not sleeping...."

Zane released a long, ragged breath. Tried to think, but his head felt as if it was filled with sump oil. She slid down onto the bench opposite, folded her hands in her lap. "You seem all right with this," he said.

"Oh, yes. More than all right." A smile, radiant with inner happiness, cut through the tension. "I've always wanted a baby."

Yeah, he remembered that. She'd wanted her ex's baby, and he couldn't keep that bitter knowledge out of his voice. "Then I guess this worked out pretty good for you."

Her gaze snapped to his. "I didn't mean to get pregnant. *I* provided the protection."

That box of condoms he'd steadily made his way through. He shook his head. "So what went wrong?"

"There's a failure rate. Only about two percent, I read somewhere. Still, they can break—"

"You don't think I'd have noticed?"

"—or if they're not put on correctly, you know, in the heat of the moment..."

In the heat of the moment. Her gaze fell away, and a flush coloured her throat, spread into her cheeks. Was she recalling his urgency? His desperation? That unbearable need, so much more intense than anything he'd ever experienced? But he couldn't believe he hadn't got the damn thing on right. He couldn't believe—

"There is another possibility."

"Another possibility," he repeated.

"Yes."

Her nervous expulsion of breath, the way she wouldn't meet his eyes, sliced through his numbness. *Another possibility.* He pictured that bloke who'd called, his eagerness to see Julia. That great goofy grin when he'd seen her coming up the street.

Why had he assumed it was his?

He jackknifed to his feet, stared down at her. "You sit there spouting failure statistics when there was someone else?"

Her eyes widened, and her face blanched, then red-
dened, as if she'd been slapped. She shook her head
slowly, disbelievingly. "I meant another way it could have
happened. That night."

He stared down at her until her gaze dropped away
again. Down to the hands twisting in her lap. "Penetration,
even briefly..." Her voice trailed away on a husky note.

Zane sat down heavily and dropped his head into his
hands. A succession of images tumbled through his mind.
That moment of total naked connection. Julia, heavy with
his child. A baby, tiny and squalling and helpless.

His baby, their baby, the result of that amazing night.

The concept was staggering. Before he could begin to
figure out how he felt, or how he should feel, or when he
might start to feel anything but this numbness, she was
talking. He noticed her tone, slow and careful and measured. He noticed her hands had stilled, no longer twisting.
He noticed her crossed fingers on both hands.

"I realize this must be a bit overwhelming, and that you
might need some time to get used to the idea, but I just
want you to know that you shouldn't feel...pressured."

Zane slowly straightened. A cold sense of premonition
tingled through him. "Pressured to do what?"

"Well, to feel like you have to offer to do the right
thing." She laughed uneasily. "That sounds as trite and
old-fashioned as my besmirched reputation, but you know
what I mean."

"You think I might feel pressured to marry you?"

"I guess that's what I was trying to say, in a roundabout
way, but I know how you feel about marriage, and I want
you to know that I don't expect that of you."

"How?"

Julia blinked.

"How do you know what I think about marriage? You haven't asked me. I haven't told you."

"That morning. After—" She shifted uneasily. "You said it wasn't on your priority list. And then, when you told me about your parents..." Julia shrugged uneasily. He wasn't making this any easier, damn him, with that hard unfathomable gaze and his cold questions. She looked down at the fingers still crossed in her lap. "You don't have to say you'll marry me just because I'm pregnant."

"I thought you wanted to get married."

Her gaze flew back to his. Her heart did a back-flip in her chest. She couldn't think of a thing to say.

"Or is it simply a case of *who* you want to marry? What if you were pregnant by one of those professional types who keep turning up on your doorstep? Would you be telling him the same story?"

"No. I mean yes!" she corrected herself quickly. "Stop confusing me! They're Chantal's idea of husband material, not mine."

"What has your sister got to do with this?"

As pitiful as it sounded, she was going to have to tell him about Mission: Marry Julia. "I thought I wanted to get married again, but I wasn't meeting any men. Chantal was helping me out, in a fashion."

"By introducing you? Like some kind of dating agency?"

He sounded so incredulous, she was afraid he might actually start laughing. How had the conversation taken this humiliating diversion? She had to get it back on track. "This is all beside the point."

"The point being?"

"I only *thought* I wanted to get married, because that felt familiar and secure." She squared her shoulders. "And because I wanted a baby."

"And now you've got that, you don't need a man?"

"I don't need a man who feels trapped."

He stared at her for a moment. "So what do you have in mind? You going to keep working sixty hours a week so you can afford to pay someone to look after this baby?"

"No!"

"How are you going to support yourself?"

"I have a little money saved and—"

"Do you have any idea how much kids cost?"

"Do you?" she shot back.

"Yeah, as a matter of fact. Gav talked about it, and you'll need more than a little tucked away." He was on his feet again, pacing. "Money aside, have you considered the other aspect of being a single mother? Having sole care of a baby, twenty-four, seven?"

Julia looked away. All she'd thought about was having a baby with Zane at her side, twenty-four, seven. How had she gotten that so wrong? She moistened her dry mouth and concentrated all her efforts on keeping her voice even, her words careful. As if they were having an ordinary, everyday conversation about how they might spend her day off, rather than the rest of their lives.

"What do you suggest? What do you want to do?"

"It's not a matter of what *I* want or what *you* want, but what the baby needs, and that's two parents living together and sharing his care, providing for him without the need for welfare and handouts. That's what a child needs."

He stopped pacing to stare down at her, hands on hips, everything about his expression fierce and uncompromising. Because he wanted the best life for his child, the kind of life he'd longed for himself, the kind of security and commitment he had been denied. Her whole being swelled with love until she thought she might burst. Her heartbeat pounded so loudly it drowned out everything but the tidal wave of optimism that surged through her veins.

But she forced herself to be still, to act calmly, rationally, unemotionally. To take this one small step at a time. "What is it you're saying, Zane?" she asked very carefully.

"We're getting married."

Eleven

Zane braced himself for her response—a flabbergasted *You're joking* seemed most likely. But she calmly folded her hands in her lap and said, "All right. We'll get married if that's what you want."

"It's not, particularly."

Not this way, not for this reason.

But what if she were smiling up at him, her eyes hazed with excitement, instead of sitting there with such grim composure? He slammed his mind shut on that thought. Julia Goodwin as his willing wife? About as likely as Mrs. H. signing on for his fan club.

What he needed was to focus. On the practicalities.

"I'll need a permanent job." Thinking out loud, he started to pace. "We'll have to decide on where."

"What do you mean?"

"We can't live out west, where I've been working. It's too isolated."

"Why can't we live here?"

He stopped pacing, stared down at her.

"Bill would give you a job in a heartbeat."

She was kidding, right?

"I know how you feel about Plenty," she continued with that same infuriating composure, "and that you haven't had time to think this through yet, but if we move somewhere else, there'll be no support network. It would be like Mitch having to bring Joshua out here, or Lisa and Gav calling you in. Think about it, Zane. My whole extended family and all my friends are hereabouts. And Kree."

She had a whole extended family and a town full of friends. He had a sister he hadn't spoken with in two months. A perfect illustration of the yawning gulf between them, a chasm he would be reminded of every day if they stayed here. He shook his head. "Maybe *you* haven't had time to think this through. You're marrying me, having *my* baby. How thrilled is Mayor Goodwin going to be with that news?"

"I don't imagine she'll be overjoyed, but she's my mother, and she'll be there for me. My parents have always supported me, no matter how much I've disappointed them."

He stared down at her. "How the hell could you ever have been a disappointment?"

"They have high standards. I had no ambition." She shrugged, as if that explained everything. It didn't.

"Go on."

"Oh, they thought the Gracey's job was beneath me, and when I married so young, that was throwing myself away. Then I didn't fight hard enough to keep my husband or to prise more money out of him. Oh, and to top it all off, I bought this dilapidated cottage at the poor end of town."

There was more than a hint of sadness in her eyes, and it stirred something deep in his gut. A place he couldn't afford to go. "Why *did* you buy this place?" he asked, focusing on somewhere he *could* go.

"I saw its potential. I loved this yard and that big old tree. And the soil is just magic for a gardener." She looked around as if taking stock, then smiled wryly. "Plus it was all I could afford."

"Because you didn't fight for a decent settlement."

Her eyes sparked. "I didn't want his money."

No. She'd only wanted his baby, and instead she was getting *his*. Great bargain.

"This is all beside the point," she said, squaring her shoulders as if with some renewed resolve. "When I married Paul, we moved from Plenty, and I hated it. I hated not knowing anyone, not having any friends or family around me. I missed the familiarity, the steady pace, stopping to chat in the street. I missed the view from the top of Quilty's and the darkness at night."

"I'm not asking you to live in a city."

"No, but you're asking me to go somewhere—you don't even know where—to find and start a new home. Don't you think that's pointless when I already own one here? When there's a chance of a job here?"

Ignoring the appeal in her eyes, Zane shook his head. "It's not an option. Bill can't afford to pay me a decent salary."

"But the business has potential to grow, and Bill must be thinking of retiring. What is he, sixty? Sixty-five?"

"Sixty-eight, and he'll die in that pit of his." He scrubbed a hand through his hair. "Look, I'm not big on working for other people. Bill would drive me nuts."

"Then why do you come back and help him out?"

"Because I owe him, all right? And it's a couple times a year at most—nothing like day-in, day-out."

End of discussion. He started pacing again, thinking about what he would have to do. Thinking out loud. "I've got money invested." A substantial amount, given that he'd never had much to spend it on. No family, no home. "Maybe I could buy a mechanic's shop." It was a more appealing option than trying to work for some other Bill in some other two-bit garage. "I'll talk to a broker, make some enquiries. Do you have any preferences—coast, inland, interstate?"

"I've told you where I think we should live."

Fine, then he would do the choosing. "I'll have to fly out west and clear up some things first."

"What kind of things?"

"I only took leave from that job—I intended returning. Everything I don't have with me is still out there."

"Oh." She seemed to consider that for a moment. "How will you bring it all back if you fly?"

"Everything doesn't amount to much. I have a mate who flies freight in and out of Price. I'll hitch a ride later in the week, after Joshua's gone."

"There's no need to delay on his account," she said evenly. "I've taken time off until Mum and Dad get back."

Now she couldn't wait to get rid of him. Wonderful. He set his jaw. "This could take a while. Couple of weeks, maybe more, depending how many businesses I decide to check out."

She nodded and looked down, studying her hands again. "Before you go, do you want to talk about the… wedding?"

The word fell clumsily from her tongue, and once spo-

ken, it seemed to hang awkwardly in the stilted silence. A
wedding. White dresses and flowers and speeches. The
good townsfolk staring and whispering and shaking their
heads.

"I mean, I don't even know if you want a church wedding or a civil ceremony, or how soon we should—"

"I don't care what kind of ceremony, and I imagine
you'd be looking for one as soon as possible."

She stiffened visibly. "As in, before I start to show?"

His gaze dropped to her lap, became snarled in images
of her soft curving belly, lush with his child. Unbidden
heat filled his loins and spilled into his veins, heat with no
outlet other than anger. "That's not what I meant, but if
you want to do it that quick, fine. Just give me a month
to get my end of things together, okay?"

Eyes sparking, she rushed to her feet. "Take your time,
but I won't be making any wedding plans until we have a
place to live."

"Having second thoughts?"

"Not yet." She lifted her chin. "But I do think *you*
should be rethinking where we live."

"Is this some sort of ultimatum? If I don't change my
mind about living in Plenty, you won't marry me?"

"No." She actually looked taken aback. "I want to
marry you, Zane."

Hope flared in his heart, as searingly quick and brilliant
as lightning, then disappeared with equal speed. Sure, she
wanted to marry him. That was why she looked so all-fire
thrilled by the prospect. That was why she'd tripped over
herself in her haste to tell him about the pregnancy.

Bitter cynicism twisted his lips. "If you want to marry
me so bad, start planning the wedding, Julia. And let me
organize where we're going to live."

* * *

He left that evening, while Julia and Joshua were down at the shops. Her resentment bit deep, but not as deep as the frustrated hurt. Damn his stubborn, inflexible, short-sighted hide. Couldn't he see that she cared? That she would live with him in the middle of the Nullarbor if that would make him happy?

It wouldn't, though.

Deep in her heart she believed he wouldn't be content, couldn't be at ease with his pride, until he faced down the shame of his past. And the only place to do that was right here in Plenty. He needed to prove himself to the people who looked down on him, but mostly he needed to prove himself *to himself*. It was a matter of both respect and self-respect.

Sadly, she had no idea how to go about convincing him.

Chantal collected Joshua the next afternoon and drove him to Sydney to meet his grandparents' plane. Without his energy, the house felt instantly flat, and Julia could only throw herself back into a grinding work routine. It filled the days. Every evening she tried to stymie the ridiculous leap of anticipation when she saw a blinking light on her answering machine.

Why would he call? He hadn't even bothered to say goodbye.

Tonight she ignored the machine's taunts and let her head loll heavily against the sofa back. Her eyes drifted closed, and she allowed her mind to float, to empty, to just *be.*

When the back door started to open she lifted six inches off the sofa. Her vacant drifting mind focused instantly. No one used the back door, no one except Zane…

…and his sister.

Julia met her halfway across the living room, flung herself into a fierce hug and promptly burst into tears. Kree laughed and blubbered and hugged her right back, and the familiarity of it, the warmth, the comfort, only brought more tears, harder and faster.

Eventually Kree managed to squirm her way free, and she stood grinning into her friend's hiccupping face. "So, okay, I know you missed me, but isn't this a bit excessive?"

Julia felt her eyes brim again and bit down on her lip.

"Hoo-kay. Shall I put the kettle on, or would you rather I break out the duty-free?" Kree lunged for a discarded carry-bag and started dragging out bottles. "What do you reckon? Feel like breaking the seal on this?" She held up a bottle of Baileys Irish Cream liqueur.

"Thanks, but no thanks." As she wiped at the tears that refused to stay put, Julia felt her friend's perceptive narrow-eyed inspection and grimaced. "I'm sorry. Hormones."

Kree put down the bottle she held with extravagant care. "Are we talking regular hormones or excessive maternal-type hormones?"

Julia flushed, and Kree blew out a long whistle of breath. "Aunty Kree, huh?"

"How on earth did you guess?"

"Come on, Jules. When have you ever been able to hide anything from me?" With a firm hand, she enticed Julia to sit, but that hand lingered on her shoulder for a long, comforting moment. "My highly tuned intuition also tells me you need to talk."

Once the words started, they spilled as rapidly as her tears, one on top of the other in a flood of emotion. At the end, when Julia took a long, shuddering breath, Kree lifted a brow. "Dare I ask if you've told *him* any of this?"

"I told him I wanted to marry him."

"But did you say *why?*" Kree shook her head. "He's a man, Jules, and worse than that, he's Zane O'Sullivan."

Julia bridled. "What is that supposed to mean?"

"It means you can't afford to be subtle, to let him guess what you're thinking. For a start, it's safe to assume he hasn't a clue that you love him. He'd think you're marrying him for the baby's sake, for propriety, for security. And that you only went after him because you were attracted to the idea of a walk on the wild side."

"Perhaps I did at first, but that was before we…" She gave a you-know-what kind of shrug. "I can't believe he couldn't feel how special…"

"Maybe he did."

"Do you think so?" Julia heard the wistful tone in her own voice, felt the optimism in her accelerated heartbeat.

"I sure *hope* so, because otherwise the two people I love most in the world are not going to end up happy."

"I know I have to talk to him, but will he believe me? How can I *prove* that I love him?"

"I don't honestly know, Jules." Kree reached over and placed a reassuring hand on hers. "But if it's worth anything, I have faith in you."

"It's worth a lot." Dry humor quirked her lips. "Although some tips would be worth more."

"Be honest and be strong. They've always been your best qualities."

"Me, strong?"

"Yeah, you, strong!"

"I'm your friend, the chicken-livered shop clerk. Are you sure you're not confusing me with someone else?"

"Heck, Jules, you don't have to be a loud, hard headed, power junkie to be strong. You have an inner strength, the kind that makes you stand firm over what you believe in."

Julia snorted.

"How about when your mother tried to make you give up this house and move in with Chantal? You just dug your toes in and refused to budge. So much more effective than ranting and raving."

"Are you saying I should dig my toes in over where we live?" she asked skeptically. "Because your brother didn't react very positively when I suggested he rethink our future home. He more or less accused me of blackmail."

"I was only demonstrating how you're not so chicken-livered when it comes to something important. If you believe where you live matters, then be strong about standing up for that belief. That's all I'm saying."

Oh, it mattered. Not because of the four walls or the big old tree out back, not even because of her family. What mattered was Zane's self-image, his ability to love himself, to be the man she knew he could be.

The longer Julia dwelled on the notion, the more certain she became. They needed to stay in Plenty. She needed to find a way to facilitate matters, and one solution shone like a beacon.

Decision made, she picked up the phone and dialled Bill's number.

Zane stood on the neatly mown verge outside her house, drinking up the familiar sights and sounds and scents as thirstily as a man returned from the desert. For five weeks he'd crisscrossed the country, chasing after For Sale signs with an escalating sense of frustration.

Not one place had felt right.

He couldn't nail down what he'd been looking for—still couldn't define it—but he'd felt it stir when he turned the corner into Bower Street. A sense of rightness that settled as warm as Julia's smile.

Weird how he could still feel it when his pulse, his nerves, every cell, jangled with anticipatory tension. He didn't even know if she would be home from work yet, but that hadn't stopped him arrowing home like some kind of heat-seeking device.

Home.

He huffed out a breath and waited for denial to bumper-smack his involuntary use of the word. Nothing. Maybe because the thought of seeing Julia again was misting every other issue. *Misting, huh!* No way that ephemeral term described his state these past three days. Ever since he'd decided to abandon his fruitless quest, he'd been one hot, tight, aching streak of tension.

And if he stood there much longer, he would be one hot, tight, aching streak of tension rooted to the verge. Whether he wanted to stay or not.

He ducked to clear the rosebush arching over her gateway, but a thorny twig snagged his sleeve. When he twisted to free himself, another caught at his back. *A message?* he wondered ruefully, reaching for his pocketknife. And just because the damn bush was being so difficult to get along with, he lopped off a couple more twigs for good measure.

A pink bud tipped his latest pruning, and he pressed his thumb into its velvety petals. The colouring, texture, scent, all reminded him of Julia. Not to mention how it had grabbed hold and refused to let go, the same way she had snared his heart.

The revelation eased comfortably into his consciousness. He loved her, and who could blame him? She was as beautiful inside as out, a rare mix of strength and tenderness, of sunshine and storm clouds. He recalled her darkening expression the afternoon he'd left, and wished he'd brought some peace offering…like flowers.

He inspected the one tiny bloom in his hand, then its mates scattered thinly through the climbing bush. The longer he studied them, the more appealing they looked. He'd cut half a dozen before he heard footsteps. The hackles rising on the back of his neck told him *neighbour from hell*.

"So, you're back," she said brusquely.

"Appears so."

"Good. Julia will be *so* pleased."

The knife slipped and skidded off his finger. Carefully he folded the blade into its handle, turned to scowl at her. "Why do you say that?"

"You have been gone a long time." A note of censure pinched her tone. Much better, Zane thought. For a second there she'd sounded almost pleased to see him. "Your sister's back, but that isn't the same as having a man around."

Dumbfounded, Zane could only stare back, but her attention had shifted to his collection of rosebuds. Dwarfed by his big hand, scrunched by his tense fingers, they didn't look so appealing anymore.

"What are you doing with those?" she asked.

Strangling them.

"If you're picking them to take to Julia, I have some late Queen Bessie's that'll do better. You wait right here."

He didn't have a clue what Queen Bessie's were, but if they rated with her cookies, he would wait. Eventually she returned bearing a huge bunch of roses and a satisfied smile.

Completely humbled, Zane shook his head. "They're perfect. Thank you."

"Nothing's too good for our Julia." She handed him the roses and placed a restraining hand on his sleeve. "You just do the right thing by her. She deserves to be happy."

Until that moment he hadn't realized why he'd returned. To make her happy. It was as simple—and as complex—as that.

Fixing Mrs. H. with a straight look, a look filled with new respect, he said, "That's my intention."

Mac heard him before he'd circled the first garden bed, and by the time he let himself through the gate in the new section of fence, the dog's excited yelps had reached fever pitch. Grinning widely, he hunkered to rub his pal's ears and felt a tingle of heat race through his whole body. His hand stopped mid-stroke. He straightened slowly.

It took him a second to find her in the shadowed doorway, but then she came the rest of the way out and let the door fall shut behind her. Myriad details skimmed through his awareness—the man-size shirt hanging to mid-thigh, hair scooped into a messy knot on top of her head, her expression still frozen with stunned surprise—before one grabbed and took hold.

Long, milk-pale legs, totally bare.

He'd rehearsed this moment a hundred times in the last five hundred miles, another dozen between the front gate and here, but the welcoming grin, the *Hell, I missed you,* the flowers and apology, were broadsided by that one inconsequential detail.

"Good look," he said slowly, eventually.

She blinked once, twice; then her head dipped as if to check out his meaning. As if she hadn't a clue *what* she was wearing or not wearing.

"I was lying down when I heard Mac going off." Her shrug looked self-conscious, diffident. "This is comfortable."

Up close it looked rumpled—*she* looked rumpled. And so breathtakingly beautiful that it took a minute for the rest

170 ZANE: THE WILD ONE

of her message to register. He frowned. "Why were you
lying down? Are you sick?"

An almost-smile teased her lips. "No. I'm pregnant."

The glow in the rich warm depths of her eyes dazzled
him. He ought to smile back; he should grab her and kiss
her until this time tomorrow, but it took all his effort to
form a few simple words. "How have you been?"

"According to Dr. Lucas, I am obscenely healthy."

"You saw Doc *Lucas?*" *Plenty's sole doctor, Doc Lucas? Her father's golfing buddy, Doc Lucas?*

"Of course. He's my doctor. He'll refer me to an ob-
stetrician later, but at the moment I only need regular
checkups."

"That's all he said?"

Her real smile threatened to break loose. "Oh, he also
mentioned that I'm having a baby around the first week of
November, and I have great child-bearing hips."

His gaze dipped before he could restrain it. *Focus, bud.
And not on those hips.* "You haven't been sick?"

"Not once. Mum said her pregnancies were the health-
iest times of her life, and the same for Auntie Lee. It probably runs in the family." One hand drifted up to cradle
her belly, and her expression turned softly contemplative.
"You know, it probably sounds really corny, but I feel
like my body's built for this. For babies."

That hand, so tenderly protective, drew him like a mag-
net. *His* hand itched to be there, resting over the place
where their baby grew. He started to reach for her, but his
arm felt ponderously heavy.

The flowers. He'd forgotten the bloody flowers.

"Oh. Are they for me?" Laughing softly she took them
from his extended hand and buried her nose in their center.
"Where on earth did you get such brilliant roses at this
time of year?"

Eyes warm, quizzical, mesmerizing, she watched him over the top of the bouquet, and Zane had to shake his head to re-engage his brain. "They're from your neighbour's garden. She's a very loyal fan."

"I know. She's seriously impressed with your fence, but you really won her over the day you looked after Joshua."

For a second a weird surreal haze blurred his mind. Mrs. H. praising him? He shook his head. "I meant a loyal fan of *yours*. That's why she gave me the flowers. For you."

"Whatever." She shrugged. "They're beautiful, and I should put them in water. Why don't you come inside and I'll put the kettle on? Have you been travelling all day?"

Reaching past her, he pressed his palm flat against the door, holding it closed. "The flowers can wait. First I have something to say."

Twelve

Turned halfway toward the door, she stilled. Her throat moved convulsively, as if she'd swallowed, and in that instant he became aware of exactly how close they stood. So close that he breathed the scent of her skin.

Warm. Musky. Woman.

Every muscle in his body contracted. Painfully. He squeezed his eyes shut and tried to concentrate on something other than leaning another six inches and burying his face, his hands, himself, in that scent. It didn't work.

When he opened his eyes she was staring at his hand—not the one flat against the door, but the one hovering inches from her body. As if he'd unconsciously started to reach for her.

"It's okay to touch me. If you want."

Her low, husky voice tempted him as surely as her inviting words. Torn, Zane hesitated. If he touched her, that would be it—no talking, no setting things right. Yet he couldn't move, couldn't bring himself to back away.

As if he were a fascinated bystander, he watched her reach for him, felt the slight tremor in her fingers as they pulled his hand inexorably closer, then pressed his palm to her belly.

"You probably can't notice any difference, but sometimes, when I'm lying in bed at night, I imagine I can feel him. Or her."

Awash with tears, her eyes met his. The concept of a tiny life evolving inside that firm flesh staggered him. He splayed his fingers, hipbone to hipbone, and imagined how she might feel in another month, another six. And his world tilted.

"You've felt movement?" he rasped. His mouth, his throat, his voice, were all sandpaper-dry.

"No—the doctor said that won't happen for another month or so. It's just a sensation that my body is...changing." A smile flickered uncertainly. "Do you...do I...feel any different?"

He swallowed. "No belly button ring."

"No."

Apart from that...hell, the thirteen weeks without touching her felt like a lifetime. And she was asking him to be objective? To clinically assess the changes? With tremendous willpower, he reclaimed his hand and shoved himself back from the door.

"I guess my waistline hasn't changed too much. It's mostly my breasts."

Her offhand words whipped through Zane's blood. He forced himself to keep his eyes steady. On her face. "How so?"

"They're tender. So tender sometimes they ache."

Ache. Oh, hell, *he* ached. Not just to peel that shirt from her skin, not only to drink in those changes, to see, to touch, to hold. He wanted more than the physical.

He wanted everything.

Struggling under the surge of emotion, enormous and elemental, he pocketed his hands in his jeans. Grimaced because that was painful. "How about we go inside? Sit down? We need to talk about a few things."

The gravity of his tone, his resolute expression, wrenched Julia from her state of sensual bliss. They needed to talk. About a few things. And she needed to be sitting to hear them.

"Okay," she agreed, but her voice sounded strangely strangled. *But please don't tell me you've changed your mind about marrying me. Please, not that.*

He waited. She stood. He gestured toward the door. And finally it registered what he was waiting for. Stiff with nervous tension, she turned and opened the door, managed to coax her legs to take her inside, but when she started for the kitchen, he stopped her.

"Leave it, Julia. Just sit."

Heart pounding, she sat. "Is this about where we're going to live?" *Please let that be it.* "Did you find somewhere?"

He shook his head, blew out a breath. "I found plenty of places, but I didn't think any of them would suit you. Us. None of them felt…right."

Us. Relief eased her taut nerves. Perhaps he hadn't changed his mind about marrying her. And he hadn't tied himself into an alternative. Hope blazed bright in her heart. "It doesn't matter, because I have some good news."

"I haven't finish—"

"I know, but I *have* to tell you this. I wanted to ring, to tell you right away, but I didn't know how to contact you. Bill, Gav, Kree—no one knew how to find you." She clasped her hands tight and hoped the effort might also hold her voice together, stop it trembling with nerves, excitement, trepidation. "I spoke to Bill about selling his business."

Silence.

"You said he'd likely die with a wrench in his hand," she continued, determined not to let his lack of response unsettle her. "But I thought, why make assumptions? Perhaps he'd like to go fishing every week instead of twice a year. And you probably think it's too small a business to support a family, but I had an accountant take a good look at the books, and while the cashflow isn't wonderful at the moment, there's a lot of potential...."

Her voice trailed off under his hard-eyed glare. What was he thinking? Apprehension churned in her stomach.

"So you're saying Bill's garage is like your cottage? A doer-upper at the poor end of town?"

"I'm saying there's growth potential. For a start, there are council contracts that go out of town. With your heavy machinery experience, you'd stand a great chance."

He made a disparaging sound. "With my new mother-in-law as mayor, I'd be a shoo-in."

"No. *No!* I didn't think that at all!"

"What did you think, Julia?" he asked, his tone ominously even. But his hard eyes glinted like steel. Hot steel. "That I wasn't capable of finding a means of supporting you? Or did you simply decide you weren't moving and you'd make your own arrangements? My wishes be damned?"

"No. I saw Bill, and I made inquiries."

"You did more than *inquire*. You checked the books!"

"Because Bill insisted," she countered. "He said I had to do that before I started getting my hopes up in the clouds."

With an effort, she paused her wild rush of words, forced herself to speak more slowly, but with no less passion. "He *wants* to sell. He *wants* to retire. A few years back he even thought about listing, but the agent was so negative about his chances, he didn't pursue it." She gazed up at him, appealing for understanding. "He let me inspect the books, but he wouldn't let me take it any further. He said he'd only deal with you, Zane."

His posture and expression remained as uncompromising as ever, and Julia had no idea if she was getting through to him. But she had to keep trying. She would keep on trying, keep on talking, until she collapsed in a hoarse, gasping heap at his feet.

"Bill thinks an awful lot of you, as a mechanic and as a man. You're the closest thing he has to family." She moistened her lips. "He even mentioned giving the business to you."

"I wouldn't take it."

Of course you wouldn't. "I told him that, and do you know what he said? 'He'll bloody well have to take it when I die!'"

Stunned eyes connected with hers. Stunned eyes no longer hard, no longer difficult to read. They pulsed with emotion.

"Now, will you please sit down? I'm sick of getting a cricked neck every time we have one of these debates."

She waited, heart in throat, as if this innocuous request—please sit—was the most important she would ever make. Perhaps it was. It felt symbolic, a chance for him to show he could give.

"Is this the way our marriage is going to be, Julia? You making decisions that affect us both, then going behind my back to set them in motion?"

"No," she said with her own quiet determination. "If

you had been here, or if I'd been able to contact you, I wouldn't have had to speak to Bill on my own."

"You didn't *have* to speak to Bill at all."

"Yes, I did."

"Because you won't live anywhere else?"

"No. And if you sit down, I'll tell you why."

For a long tense minute she thought he would stand his stubborn ground, but finally, with obvious reluctance, he sat. Call her warped, but there was something in his inflexibility, in that knock-me-over glare, that filled her heart to bursting. She imagined that love coloured her voice when she smiled at him. "I did it for you, Zane. Because I want you to be happy."

He stared at her, his expression blank, and that happy rosy glow dipped and dimmed.

"Not much of an explanation, I see."

"Why?" he asked hoarsely, eventually.

She released a long breath, stared at her hands. "I was thinking about your past, how every time you drive into Plenty you enter this time warp where all you can see is the way things used to be. All you can feel is the shame and the distrust, and that colours how you see yourself and how you see me. I don't think that will ever change unless you face up to that past. Until you prove you've outgrown it. Until you show this town the man you've become."

"What kind of man is that?"

Kree's advice whispered in her ear. *Don't be subtle. Tell him, Julia, so there's no mistake.* She squared her shoulders, lifted her chin and looked him right in those difficult-to-read eyes. "I want them to see what I see. A man whose sense of duty brings him back twice a year to a town he hates, even though his debt's been repaid twenty times over. A man who takes leave from his job to help out a mate when his wife has a new baby. A man a toddler trusts instinctively from the first 'Hey, bud.' A man who takes my breath. A man I love with all my heart.''

There she'd said it, all of it, and he sat staring back at her as if she had lost her marbles. Damn him. Unaccountably, her eyes filled with tears.

"And that's about all I have to say, except that if I didn't love you, I would never have agreed to marry you, pregnant or not. And besides that, if I didn't love you, I would never have been pregnant in the first place, because I wouldn't have slept with you.''

"Are you finished?"

Blinking away the tears, she nodded. And with clearer vision she noted he didn't look quite so stunned. Still a little dazed, but a softness she'd never seen before hazed his expression.

And she remembered one last thing. "But if Bill's business doesn't suit, then that's okay.''

"Okay, how?"

"I mean I will still marry you. I will live with you wherever you choose.''

"Even the city?"

"If *you're* there.''

And if the previous five minutes hadn't blown Zane completely away, that little shrug would surely have finished the job. *If you're there.* For a long time emotion choked any chance of reply. It welled from deep inside, a complex blend of tenderness and passion and incredulity.

Julia Goodwin loved him. What had he done to deserve this?

He knew he would do anything to keep that love alive, to make himself a better man, a respected man, a worthy man. He reached for her hands, linked his fingers through hers, cleared the huge lump from his throat.

"I don't know if Bill's business will suit me or not, but

what I do know is *you* suit me. Your house suits me. Even this miserable town is growing on me. It took me five weeks to work that out. I kept blindly searching, not even knowing what I was missing, driving on to the next place, all the while thinking something would leap out and yell, 'This is it!'

"Only one place has ever done that. I suspect it's because you're in it, but as long as you are, that's where I want to live, too."

"You do?" Her smile crawled into him, coiled around his heart.

"Didn't I just say so?"

"Is that all? Have you finished?" Softly mocking.

"No, I haven't got to the most important bit." He squeezed her fingers. "I want to do this right, but I can't do the down-on-one-knee thing yet."

Her eyes rounded. "Does it still hurt?"

"Only if I put too much pressure on it." He leaned forward, expression solemn. "I want you to be my wife, Julia. In my bed, in my life, to have and to hold, forever. Will you marry me?"

"You know I will."

"When?"

She laughed with obvious delight. "That's something we have to talk about."

"Haven't you organized it yet?" He tugged at her hands, hauling her close to his side. It wasn't close enough and she thought so, too. Her eyes sparkled contemplatively; then she slid onto his lap, straddling his thighs. His hands settled on her waist. "Much better."

"I thought seeing as I've organized where we'll live—" she traced a teasing hand down his jaw "—you could make the wedding decisions."

"Okay." He shrugged. "Tomorrow. This garden."

"I would love nothing better, but with winter coming, the garden might not be the best solution."

"We could wait till spring."

"Would that matter? I mean, I will be really...big."

"You think that's going to bother me?" He shifted one hand from her waist to cradle her belly, felt his voice thicken with emotion. "I can't wait until I feel our child here. Until I know everyone can see you carrying my child."

Eyes misting, she bit her lip. "Will you please just kiss me?"

"I don't have a problem with that."

And when he'd kissed them both breathless, he pulled back and saw that her eyes burned with the same kind of emotion he felt through his whole body. His whole being. One hand cupped his face, jaw to chin, and he felt it tremble as she acknowledged the intensity of feeling. Eyes fixed on hers, he turned his face until his lips touched her soft palm, then the inside of her wrist. He felt the kick of her pulse and the answering drum of his own.

"When I saw you in the yard, when you told me you were wearing this shirt for comfort, I couldn't help wondering what was, or wasn't, underneath."

She smiled primly. "Do you really think a good girl like me would walk out the back door with nothing under her shirt?"

He fixed her with a level gaze. "Am I about to find out?"

"I guess it's your lucky day."

"Amen to that."

Their eyes met, held, and Julia wondered how she'd ever thought his cold. Right now, as she reached for the hem of her shirt, they sparked with blue heat. Slowly she eased it upward, baring her legs, then the broad denim spread of

his thighs. They looked—they felt—incredibly erotic between hers.

"Good Girl panties." He brushed his knuckles against
a cluster of mauve daisies, and Julia dragged in a breath.

Incredibly turned on by that one simple touch, she licked
her lips and shimmied the shirt higher, over the curve of
her belly and the swell of her breasts. Then she ripped it
from her arms and tossed it behind her. She saw the dip
of his Adam's apple, the flare of his nostrils, and she felt
the singe of blue flame. Her nipples beaded against the
lace of her demi-cup bra with an intensity akin to pain.

"That is not a Good Girl bra," he rasped tightly. Then,
"It looks uncomfortable. I think you should take it off."

Her trembling fingers fumbled twice, three times, with
the tricky hooks at her back before the thing fell away.

"And your hair. It needs to be down."

When she reached up for the scrunchie, she felt the
warm rush of his exhalation. Against her bare breasts. And
then her hair swung loose, and she swore she felt the caress
of every individual strand against her oversensitized skin.

"Beautiful," he whispered.

At the first stroke of his fingertip, she closed her eyes.
When he continued to tease, a knuckle brushing the soft
underswell, a fingertip tracing the outer rum of her areola,
she fidgeted with impatience. His hands gripped her hips,
held her still, as he dragged his tongue across one nipple.

Fingers clenching in his hair, she implored him to stop
the torture, and when finally his mouth closed around her
distended nipple, she cried out with the exquisite pleasure.

His unhurried hands and generous mouth moved from
breast to throat, from shoulder to earlobe, until she thought
she might die with frustration. She reached for his jeans,
felt him suck in his stomach as she slid the button free.
The zip wasn't so easy.

"It seems to be stuck on something," she decided.

His hoarse bark of laughter didn't discourage her, and she managed to get the fastener down, to find him and free him into her hand. Strong, smooth, glistening.

"Beautiful," she whispered. "And all mine."

She touched her tongue to her top lip, and he groaned. When she startled to wiggle down, he grabbed her firmly by the waist. "Not a good idea."

"I thought it was inspired."

Laughter rumbled low in his chest, and she leaned forward to rest her cheek there, to absorb the sound. And she made a solemn promise to herself. She would make him laugh every day of his life.

"I have a better idea," he said, pulling her upright.

"Does it involve getting me out of these panties?"

"Absolutely."

"Sounds like a plan."

Naked, she scrambled back onto his lap, but he held her away while they kissed, while he gazed into her soul.

"There's something about your eyes," he murmured solemnly as he eased her over him, "that gets me every time."

"There's something about you," she murmured solemnly as he filled her with exquisite incredible pleasure, "that completes me every time."

They smiled into each other as she moved against him, as her body quickened around his silky heat, and then there was nothing but heat and sensation, and the quest to ride it to its final shuddering climax.

Spent, she collapsed against him and finally heard the words she'd craved. "I love you. I hope you know that."

She pressed a kiss to his chest and snuggled closer. "Yes, but it's about time you told me."

And she knew that *this* was what she had wanted all along. To be loved. Extravagantly, completely, unrestrainedly.

By this man. Her man. Her love.

Epilogue

It was exactly like a scene from the movies.

The action cut to slow motion as the first notes of the wedding march rang out, bringing the guests to an instant hushed stillness. The camera zoomed in for a closeup as Julia wrestled for control of her trembling limbs. As her two bridesmaids—sister and soon-to-be sister-in-law—fussed over the fall of her skirt and a stray curl of hair.

There was a sense of time standing still. A sudden clarity of thought, sound, motion.

She was about to marry the man she loved, the man who loved her, in the garden of their home on Bower Street. It was, without question, the happiest day of her life.

She smoothed a hand over the prominent curve of her belly, then tucked her fingers firmly into the crook of her father's arm.

"Ready, honey?"

Her smile glowed right from her heart. "Oh, yes, Dad. Absolutely."

When the whispers of "Here she comes" rippled through the guests, Zane dragged a deep draft of heavily fragrant air into his lungs and slowly turned. His gaze found her instantly, and the sight of her drove all that air right back out again. Gliding on her father's arm through the wild riot of plants, her full skirt lifting in a subtle shift of the breeze, she looked like some ethereal beauty born of the garden itself.

Zane's heart pounded thickly. A pall of tension seemed to race her down the aisle, to circle and settle over him like a shroud. He squeezed his eyes closed and heard the escalating murmurs of an appreciative audience, a riffle of paper as the celebrant opened her book, the soft crunch of autumn leaves under the fall of approaching feet. And when he opened his eyes she was right there, her fingers reaching for his, her smile anchoring him with its warmth and love.

"Helluva place for a wedding," he drawled as he linked his fingers with hers and took them to his lips. Julia laughed huskily and wondered if she would ever become accustomed to the impact of that smoke-and-whisky voice.

The celebrant cleared her throat. "Are we ready to begin?"

"Absolutely," they both said at once, and she felt his hand squeeze hers. Felt an overwhelming surge of love and squeezed right back.

"Absolutely," she repeated, but before the vows began, she took a minute to turn and drink it all in.

Their house, the guests, Mrs. H.'s happy tears and her

parents' pride. Kree's wink and the silent message Chantal mouthed.

Mission: Marriage—successful.

Oh, yes indeed.

* * * * *

Silhouette® Desire

presents

A brand-new miniseries about the Connellys of Chicago,
a wealthy, powerful American family tied by blood to the
royal family of the island kingdom of Altaria.
They're wealthy, powerful and rocked by
scandal, betrayal...and passion!

Look for a whole year of glamorous and
utterly romantic tales in 2002:

Silhouette®

Where love comes alive™

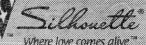